CATHERINE FORDE

EGMONT

Author's Note

I am indebted to David McColl and Rosemary
Porterfield of Strathclyde Police, and Tom Philliben,
Report Manager, Scottish Children's Reporter
administration, the three of whom answered my
questions on the criminal justice aspects of this
story with patience and clarity. Any inaccuracies in
my interpretation of their advice is wholly my fault.

For Pauline

EGMONT

We bring stories to life

First published 2006
by Egmont UK Limited
239 Kensington High Street, London W8 6SA

Copyright © 2006 Cathy Forde

The moral rights of the author have been asserted

ISBN 978 1 4052 1056 0

5 7 9 10 8 6 4

A CIP catalogue record for this title is available from the British Library

Typeset by Avon DataSet Ltd, Bidford on Avon B50 4JH
Printed and bound in Great Britain by the CPI Group

Contents

Monday

It feels weird, watching Dad drive Mum off. She's hanging out the front passenger window waving with both arms until she disappears. Yelling her head off, 'Beee goood!' No seat belt. She'd string me up for doing that, specially with Annie watching. *Terrible example to your sister.* Seeing Mum behave so unlike herself that she breaks the law, I should sense this could be a strange week.

Not that there's time to brood on how different things suddenly feel with Mum gone. I'm on duty now. Clocked on. In at the deep end. First job: keeping grip of Annie while she jackknifes to escape my arms and chase Dad's car all the way to the station.

'Muuuuummeeeeee!'

Loud enough to burst both my eardrums and blow the top of my head off, she's bawling.

'Shhhh, she'll be back soon,' I whisper into Annie's hair, coorying her close. Pinching Mum's trick in a situation like this. Harder to pull off than Mum makes it look, especially with a pair of flower-painted Doc Marten heels drumming holes in your pelvis. It gets me nowhere.

'Mummmeee! Want mummmeee,' Annie howls even louder, whacking her flying fists at my eye sockets.

For a three-year-old, she packs a mean punch, does Annie, and the shock of her attack brings tears to my eyes. Can you believe that? Bubbling? I mean, I'm turned sixteen: OK. Just. And I know I don't look it – small for my age, as thoughtful adults keep reminding me – but I'm officially old enough to mind Annie this week while Mum does some course in Leeds. Don't ask me what. Children and social justice blah-de-blah. Open University summer snore-a-thon . . . Whatever it is, Mum has to do it, else she'll never get to retrain as a social worker when Annie starts school.

'And you know that's the only reason I'm going away,' Mum said when all the details of her course arrived and it first dawned on her that I'd be better than anyone at childminding Annie. My dad, as per usual, had too many convenient problems at work to take a week off, and my gran with her bad legs wasn't fit. Mum was up to high-doh about hiring a nanny until it twigged that her own built-in Mary Poppins, aka yours truly, had been spit-spotting under her nose all along. Was Mum chuffed!

'I can relax knowing you're looking after Annie instead of some stranger. You're so good with her, Keith. I'd worry myself sick leaving Annie with anyone else, but I know I can trust you,' Mum tried to soft-soap me when I seemed a bit doubtful; *my* summer hols after all. Who wants to play mummies? Then my mummy promised, 'Of course, I'll pay you the going rate,' which kind of clinched things, since

I'm always skint. Mum buttered me up too, in case I changed my mind.

'You'll have an easy week, Keith. You're Annie's hero.'

Aye right, Mum! I'd need to be Annie's flipping Superhero, zooming from the clouds in spangly lycra and a magic cape, to stop the full-blown tantrum she's throwing now Mum's completely out of sight. Fists and sobs and tears and feet. *Just please don't puke*, I'm begging into myself, wrestling Annie towards the house before the neighbours see us and think it's me skelping her.

Funny thing is – and I'd better set the record straight, because I've not created a very good impression so far – 99.999 per cent of the time Annie's well decent. For a fem-sprog. Cute as get-out for starters. Boingy black hair everywhere like a tumbledown Afro. Dimples. Plus these teeny hands that are always smacking my leg for attention. Annie's precious too. Let's just say I've had baby sisters that never made it out the delivery room they were born in. Molly. Orla. A brother, too. Mum let me hold him and choose his name. I went for Beau. Something different, so I'd never forget. As if. The nurses took photos of us. He'd have been five this year.

So now you know why Annie's precious. Mum and Dad are always saying they're so lucky she's here. And she's so smart. So bright. Talking non-stop. 'Teef,' she calls me because she can't pronounce the 'K' or the 'th' of my name, and it cracks me up. Very first word she said – not that I'm blowing my trumpet or anything – before 'mum' or 'dad' or 'no': 'Teef.'

Now that is smart, yeah?

'Dove you, Teef,' Annie likes to say. Which proves she's not only smart, but a tot with taste.

'Dove you, Annie,' I say back.

OK, so now I've given away my deep dark secret: I'm a sammy when it comes to Annie. But I can't help it. It's not as if I'm unique. All my mates think she's quality, crowding her like flies on a cow-pat if Mum ever brings her up to school. Stewball and Stevie, my best mates (six foot plus and black belts at karate the pair of them), are dotey about her. Love her to bits. Couldn't be my mates if they didn't.

'You're dead lucky,' they're always moaning whenever I mention Annie in conversation. They crack up at everything she says and swear they'd trade in all their brothers easy for one of her. Straight swap.

In fact, Stevie went all teary-eyed when he came round last night to say cheerie before he jetted off to Portugal with his folks. Poor old him!

'Can't be assed going,' he mumped. 'Better fun chillin' here. Oh, *lovely* cake, Annie.' Stevie's top half was inside Annie's Wendy house as he grumbled all this. He wasn't even talking to me: his mate! I was left with his legs and butt for company, thinking, *Better fun chillin' here with Annie, you really mean, Stevie. You want to spend the next week pushing her swing, building her tents, being dressed up daft and bossed around until she gets bored with you and orders: 'Do home now, Tevie.'*

To tell the truth, last night, once Stevie had blown Annie the hundredth kiss and split, I'd been secretly pleased that he and Stewball (already on holiday: a Minnie Mouse postcard from Florida arrived for Annie this morning: WISH YOU WERE HERE, ANNIE. LOVE STEWBALL XXXXXXXXX – not one mention of yours truly!) weren't going to be around, fighting amongst themselves for shots of Annie.

'Just you and me,' I crept into her room and whispered after Mum sang her to sleep last night. 'We'll get on like a house on fire, won't we?'

Ten minutes into my new job and I'm wishing good old Stevie and Stewball were here after all. *Bale me out, guys.*

Annie's going ape, nearly bashing the glass out our sitting-room window frames with the flat of those cute hands I told you about.

'I want my muummee.'

What she needs, of course, is something to take

7

her mind off the gaping hole Mum has left behind for me to fill. But for once, nothing distracting is on hand. Mum's blitzed the carpet of toys, and even Raggy, the scaffy mophead doll Annie drags every-where, is AWOL. Normally one glimpse of Raggy's enough to make Annie put a sock – or rather, a thumb – in it. Even if she's throwing a mega-wobbly. Like magic, the fingers of Annie's non-thumb-sucking hand will reach out and ripple until Raggy's mophead is tangled among them. Annie's eyes glaze over at the touch. Then – ahhhh blissto! – it's peace and quiet all round . . .

Alas. No chance of that for me without Raggy.

'Nightmare,' I hear myself puff, sounding the spit of Mum whenever Annie gives it laldy. I'm sweating from the effort of pinning Annie's legs together to stop her kicking the glass. At the same time I'm looking round for something to catch Annie's eye, but everything in the room looks dull without the presence of my mum to light the house up like a twenty-four-hour sparkler.

Then something makes Annie stop crying. Instantly. Makes her rear up stiff. Give one huge gulp, then freeze.

That something is coming out of a taxi.

It has matted blue hair, all spiked up and red at the tips. Like the flames on a match-head.

'Whoa,' I say, as the blue head spins to shut the taxi door.

'Funny,' giggles Annie, splatting herself against the window to get a better look. Then she whimpers, her hand groping for mine. She buries her face in my neck.

She's been spotted by the new arrival, and a red clown-mouth is grinning at her from a face painted half black, half white. One liner-ringed eye is winking and winking at her above a cheek so thick with make-up, it's criss-crossed with peeling cracks, like a china doll that's been dropped on its head. *Gross*, I'm thinking, wondering at the same time exactly *why* this clown's skipping up our path waving two hands at Annie.

What the heck . . . ? I hear myself gulp, wondering if one of Annie's punches has concussed me and I'm hallucinating, because I don't like what I'm seeing. I mean – and I don't think I'm out on a limb here – even in a circus, clowns are freaky. I've always thought that, long before Stewball made me watch *It*, that sickoid Steven King horror about the psycho clown, and I had to sleep with my light on for weeks. Nothing funny about clowns, no matter how many times they trip each other up. Good? Evil? You never know what's going on behind the face paint. I've always thought that, so you do *not* want them anywhere near your house. Especially when they're taller, wider, beefier than you are, and dressed from head to toe in

shredded black clothes,

a studded leather collar,

steel-tipped Docs (not a flower in sight),

draped in chains.

And your kick-boxing mum's on a train halfway to Leeds and your dad's thirty miles away buried in work . . .

'It's OK, Annie,' I lie into my sister's ear, though I doubt she hears me. The blue-haired clown is rapping our window with the base of a hinged thumb-ring.

'Hel-lo,' the clown sing-songs from the other side of the glass, hunkering down to catch Annie's eye. The voice is light and friendly, but when Annie digs her head deeper into my neck, the clown face glares at me instead.

'Gonna let us in?' it says. More of a threat than a request. Accent a mix of Scottish and English.

I can't move. Can't take my eyes from the flaking face pressed up to my window. I can see zits through the patches of skin where the white make-up has crackled and flaked like old paint. This is a young guy. What's his game?

Backing off from the window with Annie constricting me tighter than Choke, Stewball's five-foot python, I can hardly think straight. I'm trying to figure if I'd be quicker phoning my dad at work or dialling the cops. As I hesitate, the clown presses his face against the window, knocking a whole knuckleful of rings against the glass.

'Oi, cloth-ears. Let us in, I said.'

Annie starts wailing. 'It's OK,' I whisper, burying my face in her hair and keeping it there. 'Daddy's coming.'

When I dare to glance back at the window, the clown's gone, only the downturned stain of his red lips and the fading imprint of his hands on the glass proving that he'd ever been there.

I still see him though. Mrs Duff's bustling him down our path and into her house next door.

That explains a lot.

'What's all this about clowns now?' Dad wants to know, his voice croaky from singing alonga every tune in the Disney songbook. If I wasn't so hungry I'd feel sorry for him. Everything he's tried to do on 'Dad's List of Instructions' since he came home from work's been a complete disaster, from carbonizing the macaroni cheese Mum left in the freezer for Annie, to forcing her to eat it so she barfed pasta all over the bath. Dad looks completely shell-shocked when he flumps downstairs to cook his own dinner. And mine. Annie's bedtime routine is usually a joint effort with Mum. By that I mean Dad pops in for five minutes just before Annie drops off and then tickles her till she's hiccupping and hyperventilating. While Mum scrapes her down off the ceiling, my dad sneaks off to catch the news before his meal's served up to him on a tray.

Tonight there's no dinner till Dad cooks it.

'Annie was hysterical up there, raving about faces looking in the windows. Spooking *me* out!' Dad sighs, garnishing my plate with a charred pineapple ring he was meant to serve cold. 'Have you been telling her horror stories today, Keith? She been watching your DVDs?'

I shake my head, grateful for any excuse to stop chewing my leathery gammon steak. Can your dad's cooking be cruelty to children?

'This freaky-looking guy turned up,' I tell Dad, using the diversion of Mrs Duff's new arrival to wheech my dinner into the bin. 'Came up our path when he saw Annie. Must've thought our house was hers.'

My dad sighs a weary whistle through his teeth, then tuts. 'Thought Mrs Duff'd stopped fostering those nutters now she's on her own,' he says, drawing his hands over his face. 'Now I'll have to get you and Annie over to Gran's for the rest of the week. Can't leave you here, and I can't get time off myself with everyone on holiday –'

'What? Gran's? No way!' I explode, and it's not to diss my gran, who's great really. Except she's got no telly, or biscuits, or space. Only an ancient fat dog called Sandy who stinks her flat out with silent-but-deadlies and growls every time Annie or I make a sudden move.

'Mum'd worry sick about Annie,' I implore Dad. 'Gran wouldn't keep Sandy locked up for the rest of the week –'

'I wouldn't tell Mum till she was back, Keith. She'd just chuck in her course and come home,' my dad interrupts. Yawning, he pushes his chair back from the table and reaches for the phone. 'Better get some stuff together. Wake madam up. I'll need to drop you round at Gran's tonight. I'm in London first thing tomorrow –'

Now it's my turn to interrupt. Worse than the prospect of five nights in a sleeping bag at Gran's with Sandy on the prowl, lumpy porridge for breakfast and no Sky music channels is the thought of all that dosh I won't be paid for childminding. I make sure my voice is full of confidence.

'Don't send us to Gran's, Dad. Annie's asleep now. It'll be mental getting her up and you know if Mum wanted Gran to look after us she'd have asked her in the first place. We'll be fine here. Honest. Anyway, it'll be better if our house isn't left empty during the day –'

I've put a mug of tea in front of my dad, filling Annie's beaker with juice to save him doing it later.

And I'm washing the dishes although that's another job on Dad's list this week. He follows me with heavy eyes for a long time before I realise I've won.

'Well, Keith, if you are staying here you know the drill,' Dad says. He lowers his eyes, nodding towards the Duffs' house. The way he taught me ages ago. 'Head down.'

Mum and Dad were always warning me about the Duffs' boys.

'All these lads have criminal records, juvenile or not. Remember that, Keith. And never mind how friendly or innocent they seem helping Mr Duff with the garden.'

Yawn, yawn. It's not as if any of the Duffs' boys would have been interested in palling up with me or Annie. None of them were ever here long enough to get to know. Two, three weeks at the most, living as part of a family before they were . . . well, 'Set free into the big bad world, God help us,' as Mum liked to say.

I'd only ever Mum's word for how friendly or innocent the Duffs' boys seemed, because over the years, I'd be at school when Mr Duff brought one back from whatever children's home had released him. 'New inmate,' I'd get in that warning tone when I came home myself, Mum describing how Mrs Duff was standing at her gate to greet her new housemate, wiping floury hands on her pinny, ready to take his bag. 'Big hearts the pair of them, taking on what they do,' Mum always said.

I'd rarely see the new arrival. Might hear him. Shouting in his room. Or at Mrs Duff. Her shouting back. Fit for him. I'd catch banging. Maybe whistling. Mr Duff's booming voice. His laugh. Sometimes, if I was in the garden, I'd hear a football driven again and again at the fence Mum and Dad put up after one of the Duffs' boys skipped the hedge we used to have and broke into our hut one night. Used Mum's secateurs on our kitchen window. Stole her handbag. Broke into Dad's car. Drove it off and crashed it.

Twelve feet high. That's a fence, yeah? And you can't see through it. It's double thick. Mr Duff complained to Dad about it when it went up, saying it denied his right to light, leaving his flower beds in shadow. Sue me then, Dad told him, well wound-up, telling Mr Duff he wouldn't have a legal leg to stand on given the carry-on we'd had over the years with his foster-yobs. Before anyone took the business to court, Mr Duff had his heart attack and pegged it. Nobody gardened in the Duffs' house any more. Our fence stayed put and the first time Mrs Duff met Dad after the funeral she told him he'd have nothing to complain about any more. She'd given up fostering now Bill was gone.

'Given up combing her hair and changing her clothes, too, by the state of her. She looks terrible,' I remember Dad telling Mum.

So this blue-haired clown is the first Duff boy I've seen for ages, let alone clocked up close.

'No worries though, Annie, we won't see him again,' I whisper when I look in on her after my first day playing mum. I lay Raggy on Annie's pillow so she'll wake up in a good mood for me tomorrow.

Tuesday

Day two and I have to say on record that this childminding lark is one total scoosh-case. Money for nothing. I mean: mid-morning already and Annie's still in the Land of Nod. With nothing to do but stack breakfast dishes. (And I've decided to wait till there's a decent pile. Dad won't notice a few extra plates when he's washing-up tonight.) I head into our garden with my ghetto blaster in one hand and one of those Seven Deadly Sins ice creams in the other. (Sloth, I think.) Well, this *is* still my summer holiday, after all, and I reckon that once Annie's batteries are recharged I won't get another break till Bob the Builder fixes it for me mid-afternoon.

'Hey, sorry about yesterday, mate.'

I've half nodded off, soaking up the sun, singing along with the spooky-sad, rain-downy section of 'Paranoid Android' when this voice cuts in some-where above me.

'You must have something better than that garbage, man? Any Prrrrodigy?'

My back's been leaning comfortably up against our fence, but it's being rocked so hard from above, I'm forced to sit forward. Squint up.

A leg appears twelve feet in the air. It eases itself over our fence, and there's this bloke – about my age, I'd say – straddling it, using his arms to take the weight of his body so the top of the wood won't dig into his crotch where it really hurts. *Crikey, there's an impressive balancing act*, the part of my brain that isn't panicking thinks. The panicking part works my vocal chords.

'You're not allowed in here.' What a dweebo I sound.

'*You're not allowed in here* – I know *that* already,' the balancing guy shoots back. 'Keep your nappy on.

22

No wonder you like Radiohead.' His voice is a sulky drone. 'Just saying sorry, mate. I know the rules. I'm going, 'case great old Aunty Duff shoots me before I'm settled in or somethin'.'

He's already swinging back over to his side of the fence. Slowly, controlled. Gymnastic. *Must be fit*, I'm thinking. Strong. And fly. He's waiting for me to say something in the little gap of time he opens as he levers himself over the fence. Waiting for me to soften. Say, *Hey, it's OK. Come back over.* Ask, *What d'you mean, great old Aunty Duff? Aren't you just here for a few days? Passing through . . .*

But I know the score, as Dad would say. Keep my head down.

Don't reply when Mrs Duff's boy says, all cocky, 'Well, you know where I live if you wanna look me up. I'm stuck here till I'm old enough to disappear. Great old Great Auntie's got me grounded.'

I don't bother introducing myself either when he says, 'Reece, by the way.' *Reeesss.* He makes the sound of his name hiss like gas leaking.

I reckon he'd have given up on me then, or at least the muscles keeping his arms on the fence would have forced him to drop back into Mrs Duff's garden, if Annie hadn't chosen that moment to shuffle into the garden looking for me.

'Teef.' Cuter than cute in her Betty Boop nightie, she's calling in this little sleepy voice, using Raggy as a sun-visor to grope towards me through the brightness.

'Hey there, gorgeous. It's you I *really* wanna see,' Reece calls down to Annie. His voice has completely changed. No more cocky wide boy. It's kind. Sing-song. Sincere too, unless he's a brilliant actor. I squint up at him. Only his head and two rows of fingers clutching the top of the fence are visible. A pale spotty face beneath a black beanie.

'Didn't mean to scare you yesterday . . . What's your name – is it Betty?'

The way Reece smiles, the way his face lights up when he looks at Annie and points at her nightie reminds me – somehow – of Stevie. This guy's smitten, hoping Annie's going to grace him with an answer.

And she giggles for him.

'Not Betty, silly *you*,' Annie says, pointing up. 'Me Annie Martin.'

'Annie. Hiya, Annie Martin, I'm your new neighbour.' Reece's smile stretches until his eyes crinkle. 'Is your dolly keeping the sun out your eyes? She must be clever.'

Annie nods proudly. 'Her Raggy,' she says. And before I can stop her she's holding the silly doll up high and switching her from side to side to show *Reeesss* where the dimwit mophead got her name.

'Snap,' says Reece, taking one hand from the fence just long enough to pluck the beanie from his head and release his own blue flame-tipped mophead like a frothing firework.

Then, to Annie's wild applause, he's gone.

'Tum back, Funny Boy,' she calls after him, clapping her hands like she's never going to stop.

* * *

Believe me, I do *everything* I can to take Annie's mind off our 'new neighbour'. Bring her inside first of all, thinking, *Should we gather up and head for Gran's? Put up with foosty cheese and farty Sandy in case this Reece guy's another of Mrs Duff's loco lodgers? No thanks*, I decide. I'll cope. After all, Reece *did* call Mrs Duff his great aunt. I'm daft thinking he's one of her regular troublemakers. Still, I lock the back door, then spend the next two hours trying to divert Annie from her new obsession by sticking every flipping animal I can think of into my three hundred verse version of 'Old McDonald'. But you know what sprogs are like once they get something in their heads. They just won't let up. I try hide and seek, animal dominoes (the most boring game in the universe), back-to-back *Balamory* on DVD (worse than the dominoes). Even make Annie pancakes and let her do her own syrup – Dad would implode at the state of the kitchen floor – but it's all in vain. Annie doesn't give two hoots about anything I have to offer.

'Funny Boy. Funny Boy. Me see Funny Boy,' she

nags and nags, yanking at the back-door handle every two minutes. Nipping my head nearly as successfully as Mum does when my room's in a state. I try to make her see sense:

'You can't play with him. He's too big.'

'Not bigger than Tevie. Not bigger than Tooball. Me see Funny Boy!'

I even hint at a darker reason why she shouldn't be talking to Reece. 'He's bad, Annie. All the boys who stay with Mrs Duff are bad,' I say, aware as I speak that I'm probably doing the guy an injustice.

That's when Annie takes her game to the next level: 'Hate you, Teef!'

Ouch!

Annie's never said anything so mean to me before, and honestly, I'm gutted by her insult. To get back in her good books, I cut her a deal.

'OK, Annie. You can say a quick hello to Funny Boy.'

Big mistake.

Annie's out our back door in a streak, giving it,

'Tum here, Funny Boy!' in her bossiest voice quicker than you can say 'young offender'. One hand is cupped to her mouth, the other makes Raggy dance. Cute as get-out – you know the way wee kids rock their bodies without moving their feet, as if they're big sunflowers blowing in a breeze? – until I try to make her come inside, that is.

'Funny Boy's gone, Annie. Let's go in.'

'Go *'way*, Teef,' she warns, giving it her Little Madam foot-stomp, so I grab her, hoik her from the fence. Then she pulls a fast one on me, clasping her arms above her head and making herself long, so she can slide through my hands like a slinky.

'Funny Boy!' she bellows, pummelling the bottom of the fence with both fists. I panic.

'Annie, Funny Boy's away. Lovely pancakes for you inside.' My voice is as close to a whisper as I can make it. Reason? I've heard something. A crackle of bushes. Snap of twigs. A chuckle. Then the rip of a match striking sandpaper. Whiff of sulphur. Reece is there. On the other side. Listening. Maybe even watching.

'Ohhhh, Annie. See you later,' the sing-song voice hisses as I bundle Annie inside.

She throws all my pancakes on the floor and jumps on them – 'Poo!' – cold-shouldering me for the rest of the afternoon. Doesn't even soften when I take her swimming, followed by McD's where I buy three Happy Meals (which neither of us touch) so that Annie won't have to wait for Stewball and Stevie to collect all the *Willy Wonka* figures they've promised to eat mad-cow burgers for.

'Want Funny Boy,' she mutters darkly to herself, forcing poor Charlie Bucket's head through the foil of her dipping sauce and covering him in fries.

No wonder I'm wiped when we finally get home. It's so late, Dad's pacing a furrow out the front garden waiting for us.

'Where have you been with her?' He grabs Annie as if I'm the Child Snatcher. 'I'd to tell your mother you'd gone to the pictures when she phoned so she wouldn't worry. What you playing at, Keith?'

Why is it you can't win with your folks sometimes? I mean, here's me, following instructions to the letter, trying to keep my nose clean, head down, avoiding the Duff boy next door, and I get grief for it. In protest, I don't touch Dad's first ever attempt at reheating a frozen lasagne, even though he hasn't burnt it and it smells like Mum's home. I storm into the garden instead. Sink into a deckchair, suddenly realising I'm so knackered that my eyes won't stay open. And to think I said this job was easy ten hours ago when I was lazing out here licking my Sloth Magnum! I flake out corrected: how Mum does this day in, day out, and then studies at night beats me.

Up above, through our open bathroom window, I hear the shower splooshing. Dad singing, 'Is this the way to Aaaaamarillo . . . ?' at the top of his voice. Annie joining in an octave higher. All these sounds seem very far away, I remember thinking, before my mind goes blank . . .

Annie, Annie, show me your Raggy, do.

I think Dad's still singing upstairs, doing his usual:

putting daft new words to old songs while he baths Annie after his shower. 'Daisy Lazy' is one of his favourites. He's totally beige when it comes to music, in case you're wondering. That'll be why I don't click out of snooze mode right away. Let the song wash over me instead, half thinking I'm making up the new lyrics in my own head.

You're so funny, I want to play with you.

Dreaming my dad's singing in that Reece guy's voice. Weird mixed-up accent: Scottish 'r's and long English vowels.

Your dolly has hair just like me
And if you will invite me
I'll give her a treat
And make her look sweet
With a punky blue hairdo.

Now, suddenly, I'm with it. Can't remember jolting awake so quickly in my life. But not quick enough, am I? Reece is folded backwards over the top of the fence, dangling from his knees, face mottled puce because it's hanging upside down, eyes bulgy. He must have gelled his blue hair rigid because it prongs out, rod-stiff, in all directions. Like a spiked helmet. One that's been dipped in blood, I think to myself. Crimson congealing on the end of every spike.

The sight of Reece freaks me out, but not nearly as much as the sight of Annie, who must have escaped from Dad while I was having my siesta. Dressed in her nightie, she's stretched against the fence, teetering on her toes to reach the tips of Reece's hair.

'Raggy want funny head,' she's calling, waving her daft doll.

'Go on. Touch it, Annie,' Reece is saying. 'Oh, but you can't reach. Hang on. I'll come down –'

'You can't!'

'Oh, oh, Annie. Mr McGrumpy's awake.'

Reece completely ignores me, although I'm charging across the garden, shouting at his upside-down face. With one stomach crunch, he levers himself up so that his hands, which had been dangling free, grip the fence. Then he back-flips down. Into our garden. Lands without a sound.

'You can't come in here,' I bleat like a flipping baa-lamb. Reece smirks at me through eyes ringed in heavy black liner.

'Annie, who's that with the shaky-quaky voice?' he asks her, in a shaky-quaky voice of his own. Face very close to hers, he cups his question into Annie's ear, pretending he doesn't want me to hear.

'Teef,' Annie whispers back, absently, her hand busy exploring Reece's jaggy mane.

'Funny head,' she giggles, tugging on his dreads.

'*Teef.*' Reece nods solemnly into Annie's face. She's way too wee to suss the mockery in his voice. 'Well, you tell *Teef* that Reece is only here because while Teef was snory-woring, you asked Reece to make Raggy's hair all blue. Like the Firestarter. See.'

Reece is up and over the fence before Annie and I know it. Back on his own side he grins down at us, balancing on his elbows, shoogling his head from side to side like it's battery-operated. Raggy's grinning down at us too, head poking out the top of Reece's ripped T-shirt.

'Give her the doll back.'

'Later. Right, Annie?' Reece makes Raggy wave at me while he speaks to Annie. 'First I'm gonna make Raggy glow. Like me. Like this.'

With one flick of a thumb, there's flame. All round Raggy's mophead. In the moment it takes for Annie's mouth to gape and shape a cry, Reece is gone.

'Don't worry, Annie,' I whisper, wheeching her inside. 'I'll get Raggy back. She'll be fine.'

Annie believes me, but I don't. I know my niggling first impressions about this guy Reece are spot on: there's something dangerous about him.

Well, things are growing complicated. To make sure Annie doesn't tell Dad about Raggy until I get her back, I decide to read her *The Tiger Who Came to Tea* in a slow drone until she conks out on my lap. I needn't have bothered. When I carry Annie upstairs I find

Dad snoring on her bed, wearing a shower-cap. Must have been there since bath time. Leaving them both in the Land of Nod, I slip out and chap Mrs Duff's door.

'Yes?'

It takes Mrs Duff ages to undo all the locks on her front door. I watch her, misshapen through the frosted glass, footering for the right key from this big bundle I've always seen clanking from a kilt pin on her skirt.

'Wait the now,' Mrs Duff grumbles. A fed-up voice, as if I've accused her of something. She jams the wrong key in the lock. Tries another one. Tuts. *Man, I'd hate to be stuck in your house if there was a fire*, I'm thinking as the door opens. Not fully. Just as far as the chain allows. A school-dinner cabbage smell wafts through the gap.

'What's the matter?'

I haven't seen Mrs Duff up close for ages. She's looking much older than I thought she was when Mr Duff was alive, yellowy pouches drooping under her eyes as if all the elastic in her skin's worn out. Her clothes are shabby: stains on her blouse, a button missing. Hairgrips escape down tails of the dark coil that Mrs Duff used to wear pinned tight as a roll of Sellotape to the back of her head. Now the hair she's tried to gather up sags at her neck like a windswept bird's nest in a winter tree, inches of white creeping across her crown. Marking the days since she gave up bothering to dye it.

Her chin juts at me, pressing against the chain while I examine her. She snaps, 'What's wrong now?'

'I . . . Annie's doll,' I begin, but I don't know how to put what I need to say. See, behind Mrs Duff at the end of the hall – a dingier, low-watt version of my own – Reece has appeared. Creeping into view on tiptoe, he signals to me. Giving it 'cut' signs by drawing a finger across his throat. If he hadn't put the same finger to his lips, then clasped his hands together, I might have thought he was threatening to slash me.

But he's begging me to be quiet.

'Doll? What doll?'

Mrs Duff's eyes narrow and disappear into their pouches, but she must have another set wide open at the back of her head, because she rasps, 'Reece Anderson. Come here.' Without turning round. Without raising her voice. 'Know anything about a doll, Reece?'

All the way down Mrs Duff's hall Reece shakes his head at me, teeth clamped together, mouth stretched wide. Pleading:

p-l-e-a-s-e s-a-y n-o-t-h-i-n-g

'Have you been pestering these people, Reece? I thought I warned you about starting your carry-on now you're living here.' Mrs Duff's voice doesn't sound fed-up any more. It's high-pitched, like a knife at the end of its tether grating down glass. Dangerous.

'N . . . n . . . no . . . Auntie Jean,' Reece begins, and maybe, after what happens later, I should have let him stammer out his lie. Let Mrs Duff deal with him. Punish him. But for some reason I'm blooming sorry for Reece, amn't I? What's he doing moving in with his great aunt? Where are his parents? Here's a guy in some kind of deepies about to get in more deepies. For what? Having a chat with a wee girl?

Me and my big heart, eh?

'Sorry, Mrs Duff. It's my fault. I threw Annie's doll over the fence by accident. Can I have it back, please?'

'If you're more careful next time,' Mrs Duff warns, already closing her door on me. She doesn't sound angry though. Just relieved. With a grim nod she sends Reece outside to lob Raggy back into our garden.

'Thanks, mate,' Reece hisses at me through the fence. 'If I don't screw the nut with duff old auntie, I'm off to a home again and the law's involved. You know how it is.'

I don't, actually, I'm thinking, swithering about whether or nor to speak my mind, and while I'm at it to ask, *Why would the law be involved with anything?* But Reece is still talking through the fence. 'I owe you one. Hope Annie likes my make-over. Get ready to catch. Three . . . two . . . one . . .'

Mrs Duff's voice cutting in on Reece is as impatient as the rattle of her keys. 'Hurry inside, Reece. I'm locking up for the night,' she orders the same moment as Raggy sails over the fence above my head and Annie spoils my catch by wandering back into our garden.

'Teef. Me want Ragg . . .' she's grizzling, sucking her thumb and holding out her free hand like the poor little match girl. She fairly perks up though, when she sees me scoop the doll from the grass. With a sleepy yelp of bliss she throws herself at it, burying her face in its mophead. Then she flings Raggy away.

'Poo. She smelly.'

I've to rescue Raggy from the sandpit. Then I nearly bin her myself. Hardly recognise her. She's charred, holes burned in her head, all the white cotton twists of her hair dyed a scummy shade of undiluted food-colouring blue and scorched at the point where they're stitched on so they shred away in blue strands when I touch them.

'Oh, oh. Poor Raggy's had an accident getting her hair done, Annie.' I'm amazed at how calm I sound, because I tell you – and I know this sounds nuts – but I want to throw up at the state of the doll. It's a total write-off; not only is her hair ruined but all her insides are hanging out underneath her denim pinafore. Reece has burnt Raggy's cotton skin away. How sick is that? I mean, Annie loves that doll so much it's almost part of her. Trashing Raggy is like . . . well, it's like hurting Annie, isn't it? I know that's what Mum would say if she saw Raggy now. Not only that, she'd spontaneously combust if she thought I'd exposed Annie to a bampot who'd do something like this.

'Poor Raggy.' Annie's bottom lip quivers. Never a good sign. I've to think fast because Dad'll freak too if he sees this carry-on. Once he's kicked up with Mrs Duff he'll have me and Annie tucked up in Gran's faster than I can say 'Sandy stinks'.

'Poor, poor, Raggy.' I gulp back my rising panic. 'But don't worry, Annie. You wait here a minute.'

I bomb up to my room. Stuff the trashed doll in the bottom of my wardrobe, out of sight. 'That's Raggy away to the doll's hospital in an ambulance, Annie,' I lie on my return. 'She might have to stay a while. But hey –' I whisper quickstyle before Annie's silent O of misery wells out in tears – 'if you go to bed now I'll buy you a new doll to play with while Raggy's getting better. Only,' I warn, 'you mustn't let Daddy see you cry because he's very tired and busy with work.' I kneel. Grip Annie's shoulders, make her look into my eyes. 'He'd be very, very angry with Funny Boy for doing this to Raggy. So you mustn't talk to Funny Boy again. He doesn't play right.'

Wednesday

All the way to Toys 'R' a Rip-Off and back I do my big-brother best to brainwash Annie. Lecture her the way Mum always lectures me about how you don't have to talk to everyone who talks to you. About how not everyone who seems decent *is* decent.

'Mum says sometimes people are plain bad, Annie,' I say. (Something I don't actually agree with myself. No one, not even the dictator or serial killer, is absolute evil. Mankind's way too complex. We're all just shades of good and bad. Well, so I think.) But is Annie listening? Who am I kidding? She's three, daft as a Kinder Surprise, and when she spots Britney, she's so excited she pees herself. Which is more than I can say for Britney. Twenty-five quid down I am, after Annie settles on this starey-eyed lump of plastic bigger than herself. A whole day's wages gone.

But I allow myself a pat on the back: Britney'll surely keep Annie's mind off Reece and buy me some time to sort Raggy out before Mum comes back asking the kind of questions mums like mine ask:

Why did Annie need a new doll?

She's got Raggy.

Where *is* Raggy?

At the market, I stop to buy one of those old-fashioned mops Gran's always using to dab the floor round Sandy's butt. Just as well. The minute we get Britney home, Annie drags her upstairs.

'Britney play with Raggy, Teef. Me want Raggy, Teef.'

There's my first dodgy moment of the day, Raggy clearly far from forgotten. Luckily, once I lay it on thick – or should I say sick – that Raggy's much too poorly for visitors, Annie's happy enough. She does, mind you, insist I turn her bedroom into a real hospital, and climb into bed next to plastic Britney. And have spots dabbed on my face with one of Mum's lipsticks.

Mum would kill me for letting Annie do that, but Dad blows me a kiss and winks – 'Hel-lo, Matron, you're doing a grand job!' – when he appears home at lunchtime to find me speaking in a high-pitched American accent (think Kerry Weaver in *ER*) with Annie's nurse's uniform pinned to my T-shirt while I listen to Britney's chest with a skipping rope.

'You bought her this doll, Keith? Out your own money? What a great big brother you've got, Annie.'

Then Dad sets me free for the rest of the day. Says the computers are on the blink in his head office so he's knocked off early because he can't think straight unless there's a keyboard in front of him. Proves his point by handing me twenty quid and telling me to get myself a pizza and a DVD.

'I want my best girl to myself,' he says, bouncing Annie out to the car on his shoulders so hard that she burps up sick on his hair. (Mum warns him every time but does he listen?)

'We're going out on the boating lake. Me, Annie and Britney. Eat your heart out, Keith,' he tells me with a sad-dad wink. Have to let him off, though. I'm in a good mood after all, because Dad's told me he's really impressed by the way I'm looking after Annie and he hasn't forced me to lie by asking if I've seen Reece today. Best of all, half my working week's over already.

Off duty, it's automatic. To slip over my back wall on to the lane that borders an area of overgrown waste ground behind our house. I do it every time Mum's not there to see, though never with Annie. Think I want to die at my mother's hand? The lane's the quickest way to Stewball's, or the shops, especially the speed I leg it. Way too nippy to clock any of the flashers Mum insists are waiting to molest me, let alone see what they're flashing. Way too fast to be mugged either, by the druggies and oddballs Mum says you always find hanging about disused paths.

Take the long way, now, Mum warns me every time I head to Stewball's. But it's daft. I mean, the only thing that's ever attacked me is one of the local dogs, out doing its business. Last time I was on my way home this big Alsatian went for my arm. Came from nowhere. Caught my wrist as I vaulted over my wall more impressively than Jonathan Edwards. Drew blood. Couldn't tell Mum of course, so I didn't get a tetanus shot. Just secret nightmares: had myself convinced I'd lockjaw.

And what do you know? The same big Alsatian's roaming the lane today; probably the familiar of Mum, keeping tabs on me. Of course, muggins here doesn't notice the dog till it's way too late. I'm merrily jogging alongside it, wondering if I should get out two DVDs – one music, one horror – when the head rears up through the weeds, cocked to one side. It's heard me. Smelt me. Seen me. Remembered me. Now it wants to taste me again.

You're supposed to stand still, so Dad tells me

whenever Sandy's backed me into the corner of Gran's hall. Show you're not afraid. Hold out your hand to let your would-be attacker smell you: *Peace, man.*

You must be joking!

I try to run, belting towards my back garden doing my Paula Radcliffe this time. No, I mean running fast, not crapping in a public place, although the way fear's tickling my sphincter it's a possibility . . . Anyway, I feel hot breath on my calf. Hear *snap!* – the dog's jaw clamping down, biting air instead. Phew! When its paws skitter on the stony surface of the lane I virtual high-five myself: *it's fallen.* Turn to check. Stupid of me, because I trip over my own size tens, don't I? Sprawl the length of myself – splat – on the ground.

There's a howl of victory. A rush of fur. Before I can get my arms up in self-defence I'm straddled by four legs and the meanest set of gnashers I've ever seen are drooling over my face.

Then it gets worse.

Out of the frying pan into the fire you could say.

Because guess who rescues me?

'Gaaa. Moosh. Gerroff my mate Teef.'

Reece uses the same sing-song voice that charmed the pants off Annie to make this killer Alsatian back off. Saunters up to the dog, swinging one of the chains he was wearing the first day I saw him. But not to hit the dog, just to distract it. No aggression whatsoever in his actions.

'Yaa. Gerroff. Ya big daft mutt! What you playing at?'

I think I'm seeing things. Reece roughing the neck of this canine killer to get a look at the collar.

'So I've to call you Lady,' Reece growls at the mutt. They're nose to nose, Lady showing she's no lady by the way she slobbers the black make-up from Reece's lips and eyes.

'I'll take her home. She's a beauty, in't you, m'Lady?' Reece says, all Cockney-mockney, kissing the dog now. 'Have a word with the owner. Don't go away, Teef.'

And here's my chance. To escape from Reece. To

scuttle over my back wall and kid on I was never here. But if you're getting the measure of yours truly by now you won't be surprised when I admit I'm still shaking like a spanner in the middle of the lane when Reece wanders back, lighting two cigarettes at once.

'Some folk treat their pets like animals. It's a sin,' he says, moving one of the cigarettes – filter stained black with lipstick – from his mouth to mine before I can tell him I don't smoke. 'No worries, though.' He yanks me to my feet, dusting me down with stinging flicks of his chain. His eyes narrow. 'Lady won't be out here again off the lead, so you're safe now, *Teef.*'

Through my coughing cloud I catch Reece's little sideways glance, the tone of his voice, and I don't feel one bit safe. But what can I do? Tell Reece to beat it when he's only after saving me from becoming a new flavour of Pedigree Chum? I should be thanking him, but I can't quite go that far. Not after what he's done to Raggy.

Yeah, yeah: I *am* working up to mentioning that.

'Are you supposed to be out? Thought you were grounded?' I begin, hoping Reece might decide to go back to Mrs Duff's in case I shop him.

'Ways and means. I slip the net. Always have, always will,' Reece says, wriggling his body like a vertical wave down to my knee height and up again without breaking his stride. He chuckles to himself, snatching the unsmoked cigarette from my fingers and sticking it behind his ear, still glowing. He nudges me, his voice sly. 'Thought all you poshies round here were meant to stay out this lane? Full of nutters, naughty boys, *bad sorts*, good old Auntie Duff says . . . Bad naughty boys like me.'

Suddenly Reece leaps in front of me, wobbling his head from side to side so that his hair dances like petals on springs. He pulls a wild stretchy face, dangling his fingers high at my eyes.

'*I'm a Firestarta,*' he hiss-sings in a Cockney accent, twirling round me in a circle so close that all his chains swing out from his body and strike me at random.

51

'Oh yeah,' I say. Unimpressed, I move beyond the reach of his chains.

'Oh yeah. *Twisted Firestarta*,' Reece echoes, falling into step beside me. Totally calm again. He speaks in his normal voice. 'Where you goin'?'

'Pizza,' I say, not having the wit to lie and head straight for home.

'Good call.' Reece scruffs the back of my neck as if I was the Alsatian. Considerably rougher though. 'Sick of old Aunty Duff's duff cookin' –'

'– She's not your real aunt.' There's no hiding the doubt in my interruption.

'Great Aunt. Late Aunt. Hate Aunt,' Reece raps, swinging stiffly to the left, then the right in time to his words. Like a clockwork punk. He introduces exaggerated shoulder shrugs. 'Something to do with my old witch of a gran up in In-ver-nesssss,' he lilts, all Highland laddie. Then growls, 'Sister. Blister. Hasn't got a mister. Who cares! I'm stuck with Duff now till I'm old enough to split the scene. Sweet Sixteen. Hot and mean.' Reece scratches an imaginary record on a turntable, then plunges his hands deep in the pocket of his baggy jeans. 'Change the subject, Teef,' he scowls in my face. 'Get us pepperoni with extra chillies.'

'You can't come with me,' I whine as he follows me into the pizza shop.

'*Why not?*' Reece whines back. 'Man,' he spreads his arms out, pouting. 'I save your life and you treat me like this. We're mates now.' When he shakes his head, the red tips of his hair brush my forehead and I shiver. See, in a way I know he's right: I *do* owe him. Still haven't thanked him. If I stand him a slice of pizza what harm can it do?

'Keith? *Come stai?* Usual?'

Mario, the pizza-shop owner, and a five-a-side mate of my dad's, doesn't lean over the counter to chuck my cheeks the way he normally does. He's too busy frowning today. Eyes moving from me to the bloke I seem to be with. Taking in everything about him. Not happy.

'You doin' all right without mamma, Keith? Being a good boy?'

Ignoring the dig in Mario's second question, I shrug. 'Margarita, please. Lots of cheese,' trying to dazzle Mario with my sunniest smile. But he's not smiling back. Reece has taken his lighter out, flicking it on and off to singe the twist of hair hanging between his eyes. Then he uses it to melt the laminated corner of one of Mario's menus.

'No mamma either, Teef,' Reece whispers in a faraway voice. At least I think that's what he whispers. His eyes are closed, he's shaking his head slowly into his chest. Gaga behaviour altogether.

'Hey, son. *Basta*. Quit.' Mario snatches the menu from Reece, who doesn't look up.

'Margarita sucks,' he scowls. 'Make it pepperoni, extra chillies.' Reece nudges me. Jerks his head up like a puppet. Cocks it to one side. Winks at Mario. Thumps his chest Tarzan-style with both fists. 'Put a fire in my belly.'

Mario's frown deepens.

'Keith?'

I gulp. Feel myself blush.

'Pepperoni.' I shrug again. Amn't hungry any more, am I?

'So. You fellas in class together, Keith?' Mario tries to meet my eyes as I pay for the pizza. Getting nowhere with me, he tries his luck on Reece. 'You new to Keith's school? Havena seen you before.'

'School?'

Reece sends the flame of his lighter shooting the length of his face. 'That's what I did at my school, long time ago, deep, deep in the valleys, boyo,' he sneers at Mario, switching – I think – to a Welsh accent. Sounds like Fireman Sam anyway. As I'm trying to work it out he whirls round to face the nearest wall as if it has spoken to him. 'So prove it. You can't, can you? You never can,' he twangs through his nose, then throws his arm round me. 'Me'n'Teef are new next-door neighbours, since you're so interested,' he challenges Mario, 'and I've just saved his life.'

* * *

'Thanks a lot,' I say.

We're back in the lane. Reece frisbees his pizza box over the nearest garden wall. Licks his fingers one by one before he replies.

'What? For saving your bacon, man? My pleasure.'

'Not that. Mario'll tell my dad about that dog going for me. I'll get hell for being in the lane. And you told him stuff. All that garbage about fire-raising. Answered all his questions. *And* said you were sent to Mrs Duff because no one else'll have you. He'll think you're one of her foster boys. We'll both be in for it.'

'Oh, I'm scared.' Reece hugs himself, pretending to shiver. Then he jumps in front of me, blocking me so I can't move on. His voice is in my ear. Quiet. But hard.

'All that garbage about fire-raising? Nothin's ever been proven. D'you think I'm stupid, Teef?' Reece leans both hands on my shoulders, squeezing. 'Chill out, man. Mario's gonna be way too busy to worry about us. Nosey old git! All those qu-*vestions*!! Vy do people keep asking me qu-*vestions*?' Reece shakes his head, slicing my face with his dreads. Then lets me go. Thuds his own forehead with the heel of his hand. Begins to dance before me, loose-jointed, every bone in his body joining in.

'*Pizza hot, hot, hot,*' Reece sings, jiggling his arms up and down like he's boneless, playing a pair of invisible maracas. In one hand his lighter flicks on and off. Too near my skin for comfort.

'Give over.' I shield my face with my arm. 'What is it with you and fire anyway?'

Reece stops dead in the lane. No song in his voice. He copies Mrs Duff's fed-up tone.

'I've told you. I'm a firestart –'

'Yeah, firestarter,' I interrupt. 'That's not *you*. That's just the name of some old song.'

'*Brilliant* song, man. *My* song. You know it?' Reece's eyes are shining like Annie's when you surprise her with a treat, the flame of his lighter reflected in both his pupils.

I shrug. 'Course I do. Song's all right. The video's

always playing on telly. It's a classic. Freaky. You're like the guy in it –'

Have *I* said the right thing?

'Oh, man. You think so. Oh, cheers.' Reece turns all coy, swinging his body from side to side, wasted as a melting marshmallow. Clearly he takes my comparison as a beefy compliment. 'You think I'm like Keith Flint? In't he the coolest dude . . . Man, I've written him *hundreds* of letters. Imagine seeing that band play live. It'd be amazin', man. Right up front so Keith can see me. *Hey, Keith*, I'd be givin' it till he looks at me. Hey. Keith. That's your name too, man . . . Wow!' Reece slaps his hand to his forehead as if some life-altering truth has just dawned on him. 'You've the same name. Keith. And you know I'm like him. And you know *my* song? It's all about me? *"I'm a Firestarta . . ."* And you know it. It's like I've come to the right place . . . It's like we're both meant to . . .'

I wish I could say I thought Reece was taking the mick the way he'd done in the pizza shop with Mario

wittering on like this, breathless words tumbling out.
A pile of mince. Back there he'd taken a big breath of
air before he answered every question Mario fired at
him, acting like a kid having a test.

'Oh, I've lived in loads of places: Liverpoooowl,
*Swan*seeee, *Buuu*minghan, Nyooo-*cassil*, Edinburgh,
ye ken ye radge? Now Glaisga' toon – Who with?
Family, if they'd have me. But they never would for
long. Homes mainly. Part of one big unwanted foster
family, boo hoo hoo –' But he wasn't messing here in
the lane. He was dead straight. Serious. Doing this
flappy thing back and forth with his hand, trying to
show there was some special link between us . . . *No
way, José*, I'm thinking.

'We're not meant to be anything. *I* don't burn
things,' I say. 'You trashed Annie's doll. That was
sick.' It's taken me till now, till I reach my back wall,
to bring up Raggy.

'*I* don't burn things either.' Reece is puzzled. For
real. 'Fire's just there. *Waiting* to start. *Telling* you to
light it. You can't stop it. It changes everything.

Specially when things are going crap –' He rubs his head, as if what I'm saying confuses him. 'Man, I thought the doll looked brilliant. All punky. Annie didn't like it? That wasn't what she wanted?'

I shake my head. Can't believe Reece doesn't understand what he's done wrong.

'Annie takes that doll to bed. It's like part of her and it stinks now. It's shredded. Disfigured –'

'Man . . . Aw, man.'

Reece could be a brilliant actor, I know, but I swear, he seems really, *really* upset that Annie's been upset about Raggy.

'I didn't mean to . . . Aw, man.'

And I definitely don't think he's acting when he turns away from me and scuds his head off the wall in front of him. 'Aw, man.'

That's when I get off my mark. Enough hanging out with the flipped-out Firestarter.

'Look, it's OK,' I tell him. 'Don't do that to yourself. I'm away in to fix the doll now. Bye.' *You're well weird. I don't want to see you again.*

Reece doesn't reply. He's still stonking his head on the wall when I drop into my own garden. I can hear the dull smacks. Bone on stone. Horrible.

'Aw, man, I'm really sorry.'

Nutter.

There's no need to sneak in my back door like this. Creep the garden path on tiptoe. No one's home. Dad's left a note on the table.

3 pm. Gone to Gran's so I don't have to cook tonight. (Don't you dare tell Mum!) Don't worry if we're late. Maybe you'll come along later?

'Sorry. I'll be in theatre,' I tell the note. My voice seems to echo back from every corner of my empty house. I can't believe how twitchy I feel, shivering as a siren wails in the distance, glancing over my shoulder to check if there's someone behind me as I climb upstairs. Daft feeling like this, but I'm spooked being in on my own. Mum's nearly always here:

humming along to my CDs in the kitchen, studying next to me at the dining-room table, rocking Annie to sleep on the sofa . . . The house feels haunted by her absence.

I shut my bedroom door on the emptiness, sticking Nirvana on loud to drown the silence. Then I set to work on Raggy.

'Thought you were never coming down, man.'

It must be two hours later. Reece is sitting in our kitchen, Docs on the table, swinging his chair that way that drives Mum ape if I do it. Don't ask me how he got in. I certainly didn't hear him, and I know for sure I locked the back door before I went up to my room. He's sneaked in somehow, and I tell you, seeing Reece large as life in my house feels like a bad dream, only this is real because dreams don't smell, do they? And I can smell Reece.

I don't know if Reece always pongs like this. Having only ever met him in the open before, I can't recall him giving off any obvious whiff. But here, in our kitchen, all the windows shut, it's overpowering. Reece stinks of petrol, the way garage forecourts do. I hate that smell. The fumes swoop straight to my stomach, flipping it, making me want to throw up.

That's why I don't say anything at first. Have to let the sickness washing over me settle. Sit down. When I look across the table at Reece, I fancy I can see the air ripple the way it does round a petrol tank being filled.

'You shouldn't be here.' My wimpy voice sounds even wimpier than before.

'Change the record, will you?' Reece shakes his blue dreads and the oily whiff of unwashed hair clashes with the petrol-fumed air. I nearly retch.

'Does Mrs Duff know you're here?'

'Only when you grass me, Teefy-boo,' Reece answers in a cry-baby voice. 'But you won't do that. We're mates.'

We're not mates. I rehearse in my head but when I open my mouth this tiny, bleaty voice speaks. 'I won't grass you, but you need to leave.'

I'm keeping my head down so I jump when Reece sends the chair he's been swinging on clattering to the floor.

'C'mon, man. Give us a break.'

Reece shakes my shoulder. Not rough, but pleadingly, the way Annie does when Mum or Dad have said 'no' to something and she tries her luck on me. Reece is pointing to Mrs Duff's.

'I hate it there. Pure braindeath, man. I'm stuck in my room. Old bitch checks me every hour. She's worse than all the house-mothers I've had put together: *Don't touch that. Don't move. Don't breathe.* Doin' my nut in, man. You're the only person I can talk to . . .'

I try not to look Reece in the eye. Know his game: playing on my sympathy. Buttering me up.

'Better get back then,' I mutter. 'You'll only have more hassle if she finds you're gone.'

'No, I'm OK for now.' He crouches down level with me so we're face to face. Whispers like we're both in on the same scam, like him being here's really my idea. He grins. Then groans, pressing his forehead with his hand. 'Told duff old Auntie I've a stoating headache and need to sleep it off. *Don't keep waking me, won't be goin' anywhere, Auntie Jean*, I told her. Anyway, look.' His weight's on me now, elbow digging into my thigh. 'I do have a headache.'

Reece draws back the dreads drooping across his face to reveal the scrapes and bruises he gave himself, bashing his napper against my garden wall.

And I should say nothing, shouldn't I? Ignore the purpling stripe on Reece's forehead. But, of course, soft lad here has to go and ask, 'What d'you do that for?' and when I hear the answer: 'Man, I'm always getting things wrong. *Someone* has to teach me a lesson,' I feel sorry for the guy, don't I?

Tell him it's OK: Raggy was only a cheap doll. Not worth banging your head over. When I'd fixed it up, Annie wouldn't notice she'd been barbecued. Even offer, muggins that I am, to show Reece the repairs I've done on Raggy so far.

Soon as I have him clumping up after me to my

room I know: this is wrong. I should be keeping Reece downstairs while I sneak off and phone Mrs Duff. Or Dad. Instead I've Reece casing my house like a bluebottle, nosing into anything that takes his fancy. Buzzing here. There. Everywhere. Yanking doors, trying windows. He opens Mum's wardrobe, then slams it shut, as if there's something in there that bites.

'Man, all her clothes are still here,' he says, backing out the bedroom shaking his dreads. In the bathroom, he scooshes Dad's aftershave all over his clothes. Tugs the medicine cupboard open, knocking over bottles to read the labels. 'Where are your dad's sleeping pills? Bet he's got loads, yeah?' he asks me. Well weird!

When he hits my room, Reece takes a run and bellyflops on my bed, tipping all the CDs in my rack to the floor. I know what he's looking for before he asks.

'Aw, no, man: Chillis, Stripes, Black Keys, Kings of Leon, Sabbath, Stones . . . You gotta have Prodigy *somewhere*, man. Duff Auntie's not allowed to give me any music. Going out of my head without it.'

I can see that, I think, wondering who exactly's giving Mrs Duff her orders about Reece. I'm scared to ask, watching my CD collection skiting to all four corners of the room. Quickly, I pull Raggy from my wardrobe.

'Aw, man, she's like a burst sausage,' groans Reece. He grabs the doll from me, holding her upside down, her pinafore over her face. He prods at the skin grafts I've given Raggy's body courtesy of a pair of my mum's good tights.

'Look at that crap stitchin'. Look at her head now. You've stuck a mop on it.'

'She *is* a rag doll. And someone *did* burn all her hair off.' No wonder I sound mumpy. Two hours I was sewing. Thumb holeyer than a tea-strainer. Now the guy responsible has the cheek to slag my handiwork!

'C'mon, man. This is why I came to see you. Been thinkin'. Wanna get Annie a new doll. Now. Before duff Auntie susses I'm gone and calls in the Reece Police.'

* * *

I don't believe I'm doing this, I think to myself as I scramble over my wall into the back lane again. With Reece. I have to console myself with the thought that at least he's out of my house. Enlisting my help in finding Annie a new rag doll.

Notice I'm not saying *buying* a new rag doll, although that's what I assume we're doing when Reece makes me take him to the fanciest toyshop I know.

'Don't know all the posh places round here, man. Places I've lived before are always on the wrong side of town. Where all the bad boys live.'

'Bad boy.' I scrunch Reece's words up with a laugh, like I'm throwing them away because they're rubbish. I'm fishing really. And Reece bites.

'Bad boy.'

He leaps in front of me, same way as he did before, doing his loopy Firestarter dance. All knees and fingers and elbows.

'Why you a bad boy, then?' I do my best to sound throwaway, consulting my watch, arranging my hoody round my waist, dead casual. Kidding on I'm only half listening. 'Course, I'm all ears.

Reece stops me dead, tapping my arm like a conductor poised to strike up the orchestra with his baton. We're half in, half out the door of the fanciest toyshop I can think of. Reece clears his throat, loud enough for the two salesgirls gabbing at the till to give us the once over.

'Reece Anderson,' he intones in a deep bass. Posh English accent. 'This is my London caseworker, by the way. Dickwit,' he interrupts in his own voice, looking at me over a pair of imaginary reading glasses, 'has a long-standing obsession with fire which suggests he could be a danger to the public and to himself. We suspect him of involvement in several cases of arson, resulting, on one occasion, in loss of human life. Unfortunately, we have no proof of Reece's culpability. When confronted with our suspicions, Reece displays no emotion. In our view he should be closely monitored by Social Services and should receive psychiatric counselling.'

Reece finishes his speech and makes me a grand bow, so low that the red tips of his hair sweep the ground. My brain has just about caught the gist of everything he's spouted, although there's no time to ask Reece to explain anything in more detail. He jerks upright to laugh wide in my face. A loony guffaw that has the toyshop salesgirls well twitchy.

'Bollocks!' he says, in his own voice. 'What's dangerousssss about me?' He pirouettes into the shop on tiptoes, arms clasped above his head, cheeks sucked in, me trotting in his wake. 'Rag dolls, doll-face?' he asks one of the gawping assistants, speaking in a high camp voice now, telling me as we're led to a shelf of Raggy lookalikes, 'Now, Cecil, remember we're not actually *buying* today. Mummy just wants us to pick out a new dolly for Tabitha, and driver will pay and collect it later in the Rolls.'

'What was all that Tabitha crap? I'd enough money for the doll we chose. Why d'you pull me outside?'

Reece had made me quit the toyshop quickstyle,

hauling me two blocks before he'd let go or speak. Now that he's standing still, I try to shrug his hand from my arm.

'Snobby tarts, following us round like that. *Anything you're looking for specifically, lads?'* Reece spits out his cigarette and grinds the stub into the pavement with his heel.

'Well, you can't smoke in shops.'

'*Can't smoke in shops.* Says who?'

'Come on. You were flicking sparks everywhere with all those soft toys about. Could have started a . . .' I've spoken without thinking. I get thinking all right though when I see the look on Reece's face.

'Yeah, sparks! Place would go right up. Whooshhh! Beast! Beautiful.' He sighs. Faraway smile on his face. That's enough for me.

'I'm off,' I say. Lie. 'Meeting a mate.' Wishful thinking, but at least Reece buys it.

'Boo! Don't weev me, Teef,' he simpers, then crows. 'See ya, wouldn't wanna be ya.' He's prancing round me again, all arms and fingers, making it difficult for me to move away. Suddenly he lunges for me, reaching a hand towards my ear. 'Oh, what's this?' he says, drawing his arm back. 'Naughty, naughty Teef.'

He dances backwards, wagging his finger at me. On my shoulder flops the rag doll we'd been looking at in the shop. Marianna, Reece had called her. Said it was after his sister.

No wonder I'm sick with panic as I head home. The long way. No lane. I feel completely trapped in a situation I don't want to be in but don't know how to get out of without landing a guy who, let's face it, has way more to lose than I have, right in it. I didn't even *see* Reece steal the doll.

All I know is that I didn't nick it, but I have it now, stuffed down my T-shirt. I want to take Marianna back to the shop. Explain there's been a crazy mistake. Offer to pay. But who's going to believe me? When you're my age everyone automatically thinks you're up to all sorts, so you never get the benefit of the doubt. Another option is to tell Dad what's happened, ask him to fix things for me, but then I'd be grassing up Reece. I'm sure the grief I'd land would be nothing compared to his punishment for escaping Mrs Duff's to do a spot of shoplifting.

I'm so lost in misery I nearly walk past the precinct where Mario's shop is before I remember I've forgotten to wave in at him, pulling a daft face as usual.

Mario's is burnt down. It's a shell. Still smoking. The shopfront gaping like a big ugly sore behind those red and white tapes that flap a warning when you pass: DANGER. KEEP OUT.

Beyond the tape, two figures crouch over a blackened canister. The first, in a noddy suit and wellies, is snapping on a rubber glove, while the other, a firefighter in a white helmet, turns over the canister with her pen. Writes notes on a clipboard.

I stare at the scene, shivering, the way you do when you've had a bad fright, maybe seen a car crash, or someone collapsed on a pavement. There's petrol fumes in the air, and my stomach lurches. Reece's voice floods my head like icy water: *Mario's gonna be way too busy to worry about us*.

Us.

Not me. I've done nothing. Don't know if he has either, but I can't help it: I'm sick with responsibility. That's it, I promise myself when I reach home. I'm never speaking to Reece Anderson again. If he comes near me or Annie, I'm getting Dad.

I stuff the money for stolen Marianna in an envelope, sticking in a note saying my friend lifted the doll by mistake, thinking I'd bought it (Yeah, right! *We* believe you . . .!), when the phone rings.

'Come on, tell me all the horror stories,' is how Mum kicks off our conversation, which has me wondering if her claim of being telepathic where her children are concerned isn't a wind-up.

I can't speak to her properly, all stuttery, hiding the Marianna money in my pocket while I'm talking down the phone, face scorching. I shove the stolen doll itself under a cushion, like we've a video

74

conference going on. Mum immediately homes in on the fact that I'm not my usual chipper self.

'What's the matter, Keith? You sound upset,' she asks, upset herself now. Worried. 'Annie all right? Dad?'

'Fine. They're both at Gran's,' I say, telling the truth, and nothing but the truth. Afraid to say any more in case everything that's happened since Mum left spills out in one big mess. On the line between us a silence blossoms and grows. Unusual that, because Mum and I don't have silences. She's not that kind of mum. We just talk about everything, and anything, always have done, and the fact that we're not talking normally now makes me realize than I'm probably missing her more than Annie is. I'd have talked my way free of the Reece situation long before now if Mum was here. Instead I'm left cringing into the receiver having fobbed Mum off – 'Sorry, Mum, gotta go. I've left toast burning. Love you!' – seeing the puzzled worry on her face as clear as if there was a tele-cam in my hand.

* * *

If Mum tries to phone me back – and I'm sure she does – I miss the call. At least I manage to post the money for the nicked doll through the toyshop door. Another day's wages gone. But one problem solved, I console myself, actually feeling quite chuffed on the way back home. Cheerier than I was when I left the house, anyway. Until I reach my street. There's a police car parked outside *our* house.

I *still* know I've done nothing, but all the same I want to run. The boys in blue are likely waiting in the front room with Dad. Three sets of arms folded: *Know anything about Mario's burning down, sonny? We heard you were in there earlier.*

'Aye, aye, Keith. Up to no good?'

I'm too busy imagining Dad's grim face greeting me inside to hear his car drive up behind me. Dad's all smiles, leaning out the window, joking with Annie, strapped into her car seat in the back. 'Oh dear! Has Keith been a bad boy while we've been at Granny's, Annie? Out robbing banks again.'

To avoid answering, I open Annie's door, unclip her, feeling better than I've felt all day the minute she coils her arms around my neck.

'Wonder what the cops are doing here now?' Dad says to no one in particular, opening our front door. He and Mum were always asking each other the same question when one of the Duffs' foster boys used to get a visit. I'd ask it myself, though none of us ever got answers.

I'm just about inside our house with Annie when Mrs Duff's door opens and two cops appear. Reece is between them, in full make-up, though done up more like a walking chessboard than a clown, black and white squares painted all over his cheeks. He's wearing his blue hair in four cheeky school-girl bunches, would you believe. I wouldn't say he looks particularly bothered that each cop has a grip of his wrist. In fact, he seems pretty cheery, rocking his head from side to side like he's listening to something on invisible headphones. Cheerier still when Annie lets go of my neck, and runs to wrap her arms round his chain-draped legs.

'Funny Boy! Me dove you!'

'Tricky lad, that,' says Mrs Duff, nodding after the departing police car. This is the first time she's spoken properly to Dad since Mr Duff died.

Dad waits until the police car's completely out of sight before he turns to Mrs Duff himself. 'How does a tricky lad like that know my daughter so well?' Dad's voice is fierce through gritted teeth, his arms locked tight around Annie's back. The glare he throws withers me as well as Mrs Duff.

'Reece climbed up the fence,' I start to explain. 'Said sorry to Annie for scaring her when he arrived at first. He was that clown I told you about, remember? Freaked her out when he came up to the window but when he talked to her in the garden she thought he was funny –'

Dad's raised voice cuts me off. 'And you *let* him talk to her, Keith? Didn't think about telling me? After everything your mother and I have –' Too exasperated to continue with me, Dad trains his sights on Mrs Duff. 'What was the boy doing climbing my fence?'

Mrs Duff holds out her arms then drops them to her sides. She sighs, slouched as though she's carrying a great weight. Shakes her head slowly.

'Tricky lad, that,' she repeats, then gives Dad an almost guilty shrug.

'He's my great nephew,' she admits. 'That's why I said I'd take him. There's no one else in the family. I've got the experience, and time on my hands these days since . . .' Mrs Duff's voice trails. She looks beyond Dad, towards the route the police car has taken Reece, though I know she isn't seeing down our road. 'Reece has all sorts of problems,' she continues in a faraway voice. Absently she reaches out to stroke Annie's cheek, giving Dad an apologetic smile. 'He lost a sister. My Bill would have sorted him. The police and social work know he's got this obsession about fire. Burning. Can't see the harm in it. He's one of these lads that've slipped through the net. Passed from pillar to post, different children's homes. Kept running away, sleeping rough. Getting himself into bother because he can't help himself. I'm trying to give him a bit of stability. Look after him the way Bill and I used to manage all our boys. It might settle –'

'Doesn't look like it so far, does it?' Dad cuts Mrs Duff dead before she can say any more. He turns his back on her. Slams into our house, ordering me to follow with a jerk of the head. Mean of him, I'm thinking. After all, Mrs Duff was only doing her best.

Thursday

The second Dad's alarm goes off this morning, he shuffles into my room.

Starts ranting on and on. Exactly from where he left off last night.

'– so just remember, Keith, you don't give a lad like that a chance. Understand?'

Over and over and *over* he repeats the same warnings about Reece until I think he's never going to work. *Finally*, when he shuts up, he rises from where he's been sitting at the bottom of my bed. Not realising he'd parked himself on the exact spot where Reece had been a couple of hours ago.

I'm surprised it wasn't still warm.

More surprised Dad hasn't caught the lingering smell of Reece's fags.

I'd been having a rotten dream, cycling along this path and my bike wouldn't steer right. Wobbly, like the nuts on the front wheel were loose and it was going to fall off. The wheel wasn't even turning proper circles. It seemed to have gone soft, as if the spokes had melted, and I could feel myself rising up and down in the saddle, same as you do on a merry-go-round. My hands were tight on the handlebars, working to stay upright. But it was hard going. Especially with Annie swaying on her kiddie seat at my back, throwing my balance out.

Then the path narrowed, becoming more like a ridge, falling away steeply on both sides. I sweated in my efforts to control the bike, but Annie – she wasn't bothered. Too busy singing, *Daisy lazy, give me your answer do,* in my dad's voice, arms stretched out like airplane wings, flinging her weight from side to side. I'd called out over my shoulder: 'Sit still, Annie, or we'll fall,' but she ignored me. I felt her shoogle the bike deliberately, and suddenly we lurched to the left, the wonky wheel skidding from under me, tipping me headlong into free-fall.

'*Annnniiieeee . . .*'

Rushing air had sucked my cry away as I plunged and tumbled, scrambling mid-air in a cartoon *Yikes!*-moment to turn and see if Annie was all right. There she was, on the top of the ridge looking down, still strapped into the bike. She was crying, arms stretching for me, shrinking from the person who had taken my place in the saddle.

'Nooooooo!'

Still falling in the slow soup of my dream, I yelled at the clown face grinning down at me, mouth painted black. But Reece pedalled away with my sister. And I landed with one of those freaky sleep jerks that scare you so much, you wake.

Crikey Mikey! The state I was in. Overwhelmed with a sense of danger. Sweating buckets. Shivering. Hot and cold. Mainly cold. Especially when I eased myself up to sit. My room felt chilled. Well, it would, wouldn't it, with the window wide open?

'Wotcha! Who's a noisy sleeper then?'

Five o'clock this morning and Reece Anderson was sitting at the foot of my bed, chains clanking as he dug his fists into my mattress, so my legs were pinned. His face was still made up in chessboard squares but all its lines were smudged grey and wonky. His bunches drooped. Mouth painted black like in my dream. I couldn't tell how long he'd been there, but my light was on and the fag in his hand was smoked to the stub.

'How d'you get in?'

Dumb question. What I really wanted to do was shout, 'Daaaad!!!'

'How did I get in, Teef?' Reece stroked his painted chin thoughtfully, then tapped his nose. 'Ways and means,' he grinned, not bothering to keep his voice down, although he moved closer until his cracked two-tone face was nearly touching mine. His breath smelt sour. 'What d'you tell them?' There wasn't a trace of pleasantness behind the black smile slashing his face from cheek to cheek.

'Tell who?'

'Anyone,' Reece snapped, waving his arms in a wide circle. 'Accusin' me of burning, everyone is. Cops wanna do me for that pizza place. Say they've got my prints, but I know they haven't. I'm in for more interviews tomorrow. Did you grass me up?'

'What pizza place? Mario's?'

I kidded on I didn't know what Reece was on about. But both my questions were accusations in disguise. Reece seemed to think hard before he answered me, turning his face away. Frowning. That's when I sussed two things about him: he'd done Mario's all right. And he wasn't near as smart as he thought he was.

'Sure you didn't grass me, man?'

Reece's eyes narrowed to black crosses, but his voice was softer. 'Duff Auntie told the cops I've been slippin' out, hasslin' the neighbours. How would she know that?'

I had to laugh. 'Duh! She'll have seen you. You're always doing it.'

'No, man. I cover my tracks. Always cover my tracks. Expert.' Reece shook his head in doubt, mumbling to himself. Dead serious now. He lit another cigarette, keeping the column of flame on his lighter going long after he needed to. Gazing into it. Doolally-faced.

Mrs Duff's weary voice came into my head: 'He's got this obsession about fire. Burning. Can't see the harm in it.'

I gulped. 'Look, you can't smoke in here. I'll need to tell my dad if you don't leave –'

Reece stopped me saying any more by laying the span of his hand against my chest, but I'd be lying if I said there was any violence in his touch. 'Man, I'm only here to jaw with you. See.' Reece arrowed his cigarette into the night through my open window. He slumped deep on the edge of my bed, drawing his hands down his face, streaking the streaks. 'I'm knackered but I can't sleep. Nothin' but grief for hours: cops, old Auntie Duffer, Doctor Pugh . . .'

'Who?'

Reece screwed a finger to his temple. 'On a mission to prove I'm nuts, not bad.'

'Psychiatrist?' Mrs Duff hadn't mentioned *that* one.

'So *she* says. You wanna see her.' Reece batted my question away. 'Total fruitloop herself, man.' He stuck his top teeth over his bottom lip, spluttering in a soft, Welsh accent: 'Now, Reece, take yourself back to the moment when the fire speaks to you, pet. No one's angry, remember. We just want to help you.' Still speaking gently, Reece rose. Drawing himself up to his full height, he aimed a vicious kick at the door of my wardrobe. And another. The aftershock rang through my sleeping house.

'Shurrup. You'll waken Annie,' I hissed. And, yes, if you want to know: I *was* spooked by the sudden violence he'd unleashed.

'Annie? Score!' Reece beamed over his shoulder at me, mid-kick. 'Might not see her again after tomorrow if the cops nail me. Which is her room? '

He'd my door open already. I'd to leap from my pit. Haul him back by his biggest chain. 'You can't see her. She's asleep.'

'Gerroff,' Reece growled, way meaner than he'd spoken to Lady Killer in the lane. 'What's your problem, Teef?'

'Just go. Now.' I'd raised my voice. Too loud. Or maybe Reece's kick had done it. Annie cried out, 'Muuuum.'

'Now you'll really need to go,' I tried to threaten Reece through clenched jaws. 'I have to check Annie before Dad wakes. He'll kill me if he sees you. Kill you too.'

I was wasting my time, wasn't I? Reece was already halfway out my room.

'Let *me* check Annie,' he was saying over his shoulder. Completely serious.

'No way!' I pinned my door shut with my foot, Reece tugging the handle. Through the wall, Annie wailed bitterly: 'Muuummmeee.'

At the sound of Annie's voice, Reece nearly

ripped the handle off. 'Don't let her cry for her mum like that, man. I can cheer her up.'

Reece hissed so fiercely through his teeth that I can't believe Dad, shuffling past my door in a mumble of sleep – "S'OK, Annie, Daddy's coming' – didn't hear him.

'Please go!' I jabbed at the window. 'Dad'll have you lifted if he finds you.' I hesitated. Gulped, then bluffed, 'When the police took you away he made Mrs Duff tell us about you. He thinks you're dangerous.'

Reece was only half listening. He'd his ear to my door.

'Yeah, well. Y'know what thought does. Nothing's ever proved.' Reece shrugged mysteriously, closing his eyes. 'And I don't mean bad things to happen. That's the one problem. Can't stop fire when it gets going. Tells you to light it, then you have to keep watching. Cos it takes your mind off *everything*.' Reece's voice was scarcely a whisper. He was smiling. 'She's not crying any more. Poor little thing. I could've helped her. I know what she feels like.'

'Annie's fine. She just cries. It's normal.' I was really losing patience now. 'Can you go now, please?'

Reece didn't move.

'I woke crying like that too. Years, I did.' Reece rubbed his hands so hard over his face that what remained of his make-up wiped away. Wan, spotty skin appeared, turning him into the teenage guy he is. Younger than I am. 'Still wake up,' he said, with a shrug that made his chains clank. 'Bet you do too, but you don't like to say.'

'Only when someone breaks into my room,' I muttered, but Reece wasn't listening. Putting his ear to the door again, he nodded to himself. Satisfied. 'She's OK for now.'

Of his own accord, Reece headed for my window. 'No one ever came for me. Pugh'll be laying that on thick when we talk to the police tomorrow. *Looking for something to take his mind off the loss of his mother.*' Reece had the goofy Welsh accent on again. He climbed outside. All fours, crouched on my window ledge, careless as a cat. The sill was way narrow for the size of him; lean back too far and he'd topple into the night.

'Bollocks! There's nothin' wrong with me. You know that, Teef. That's why we're mates, yeah?' He swayed for a moment, leering in my face before he lunged sideways for the nearest downpipe.

'If I don't see you again, say hi to Annie for me. Cops are saying they'll throw away the key if they can pin me for Mr Pepperoni's place.'

'Yessss! You're leaving.'

It took some willpower not to punch the air as I locked my window on Reece, triple-checking it before I went back to bed. Mates! Who's he kidding?

So Reece is out of my hair. Today at least. Maybe for good if he's charged with burning Mario's. This whole business could even be over *now* without Dad or me ever having to tell Mum about it.

Why then do I feel as bad as I do on this, the

second-last full day of being Annie's childminder? Mum'll be home Saturday morning. Stevie on Sunday.

Yet I'm a complete misery guts. No time for Annie, plonking her in front of the real, celluloid Mary Poppins because I can't be bothered with the toys' picnic I promised her last night, using the pouring rain outside as a mean excuse.

'Too wet for the garden. We'll have the picnic another day.'

We were supposed to be baking mini cakes and biscuits. I'd said I'd write proper invites to all Annie's teddies and dolls, sticking on her Postman Pat hat to deliver them: 'Come and meet Britney.' It's the kind of thing Stewball, Stevie and I would end up getting right into (I know, we should get a life. We do associate with girls our own age, too, I'd like to state here, for the record), making sure Annie's plastic teaset was set up just the way she likes it. We'd probably have dressed up as butlers for the occasion just to see the look on Annie's face; Stewball with his video set up, filming it all to show Mum later. But today. Oh, I don't know what's up with me.

Well, I do.

Reece Anderson. OK, he's gone, possibly for good after what he said last night, but he won't go away. I feel his presence weighing me down like one of those lead aprons the dentist makes you wear when you get an X-ray. Try shaking that off, and getting on with things as normal, when it's pressing, a reminder of all the things I know now that I'd rather I didn't.

Reece petrolled Mario's.

He's a firestarter.

He's dangerous.

He can't tell right from wrong.

I had him in this house last night.

I've let him play with Annie.

He thinks we're mates.

And I can't help feeling sorry for him.

Dad's constant phone calls don't make me feel any better. Every hour he's on the blower: 'No sign of you-know-who next door? Good. Just remember if you do see him: head down; he's trouble.'

Annie's even worse: 'If you not play with me, me make Funny Boy play with me.'

I keep telling her, 'Look, Funny Boy's gone, Annie. Just forget about him.'

What a hypocrite, ordering a three-year-old to do what I can't do myself.

I lean my arms against our fence, rain streaming down my arms and neck long after Annie has given up on Funny Boy answering her and toddled inside with Britney. I know Reece'll only begin to work his way out of my system if he doesn't come back tonight. Until then he's like a sickness bug taking hold of me, affecting every particle of my mind and body. You know what those bugs are like? They make you feel worse before you start to feel better. Only rarely do they fade away by themselves. It's a waiting game.

The longest day of my week so far, I don't know how I'm going to get through it. I'm back and forward checking every car that drives into our crescent, clockwatching for Dad to come home. Desperate, I am, for him to take over with Annie so I can slip upstairs to sleep Thursday out into Friday.

Who am I kidding? When I *do* get to my bed, pleading exhaustion when Dad comes home, how can I sleep? How can I crash out when every nerve in my body's jangling? Without having the distraction of Annie to look after, I'm even more wired for the first hint of a vehicle drawing up outside. I'm rehearsing all the possible options: if it's a taxi, if only one door slams, if Mrs Duff's alone . . . well, that would be the best-case scenario. Too good to be true, knowing my luck.

If a van pulls up, or a police car. If I hear several voices . . .

Then he's back.

Over and over I find myself whispering the worst thing that can happen – *he's back*. It's as if I'm trying to prepare myself so I won't freak out when I know for sure that Reece is still going to be around.

He's back. He's back. And I won't be able to keep him away.

I must actually be chanting the worst-case scenario louder than I think, because I don't even hear the car pull up outside when it does arrive. Only Reece, his sing-song voice ricocheting from the facade of every house in our crescent.

'Honey, I'm home!'

'Shhhh, will you. You'll wake the neighbours,' Mrs Duff scolds, her voice dragged-down weary.

'It's very late,' a different woman adds. Could be a Welsh accent. 'I won't come in, Mrs Duff. I'll pick you up Saturday, Reece, and we'll drive to Rankin House. You be packed up for me. Try to be good, now,' she calls over the sound of an engine pulling away.

Dad's already pelting upstairs to my room. To avoid another lecture, I pretend I'm out for the count, snoring. He shakes me anyway.

'Keith, that clown fella's back. Just seen him walk up Mrs Duff's path on his hands.'

But – if I've heard right – it sounds like he's on the

move again. Only here till Saturday, and Mum'll be back then, which means Annie won't give two hoots about her Funny Boy any more. *Sweet,* I celebrate to myself, trying to ignore the nagging sleeve-tug of pity I've felt for Reece since I first saw him. *Where's he going now? How's he going to end up?* Instead I focus on Dad, who repeats all the same warnings which began this long day. I let him rant. I'm feeling much better.

So much better I kid myself that things won't come to a head.

Friday

'Keith.'

'Dad. Everything's *fine*.'

Late morning. Phone call number six from Dad.
Can you blame me winding him up a bit?

'Firestarter and I are playing with Annie. Burning
cushions right now. I'm gonna nip out for some more
matches, but it's OK; Reece'll look after Annie –' I
begin, all smart-ass sarky because I'm feeling much
better than I did yesterday. Don't stop talking to give
Dad the chance to bring me down with yet another
gloomsville warning about our naughty neighbour.
After all, I'm not planning on seeing him again,
am I?

'Nah, kidding about Reece,' I go on, because I

suspect Dad's having an apoplectic fit from the loaded silence on the other end of the line. 'Annie and I are tidying the place up for Mum coming back. Gonna paint a Welcome Home banner. Won't be outside unless the rain goes off. You don't need to keep phoning me –'

'– Keith!'

Dad has to shout to cut in. His voice is tight. 'Listen, will you? There's a problem. I'm at the airport waiting for a flight to Manchester. Computers are down again in head office. The fella that deals with it down there's on holiday so they need me. Can you hold the fort with Annie till I get hold of Gran? You'll probably have to stay there tonight.'

I groan. 'You don't know when you'll be home?' How many times have I heard Mum ask Dad the same question, knowing by the way her voice turns small that she's not completely happy? Even if, like me, her words make everything sound fine:

'Yeah, course we'll be OK, Dad.'

'Yeah, I'll keep trying Gran.'

'Yeah, I know you have to go.'

'No, I won't talk to Reece.'

'We'll be fine.'

Annie and I are fine actually – at first – throwing ourselves into making the house look the way Mum left it at the beginning of the week. I hoover every room, hearing myself ask out loud more than once where all these crumbs come from (just like Mum). I force the drone of the machine to drown the anxiety which creeps up on me whenever I start wondering if I really *will* cope here on my own without Mum and Dad. Would I be better going to Gran's? When Reece is next door. His very last night.

While I hoover, Annie's in charge of dusting. Or rather, she's in control of Mum's industrial-sized tin of Mister Sheen. She positions herself in the middle of each room, then sprays every surface as if she's Lara Croft holding one of those paintball guns. By the time I've mopped up all the puddles of polish she's skooshed on Mum's good furniture, we're halfway through the afternoon. Haven't even stopped for lunch, because we went from hoovering to banner-making (should have left any clearing-up until Annie was done finger-painting, shouldn't I?). Even the rain's off: the sun is out, the sky is blue, as the old song goes. Better than that, there's been no sign of Reece, and Annie hasn't mentioned Funny Boy's name once. Not a cloud to spoil the view, in other words.

I relax. Unlock the back door. Fling it open. Breathe in the smell of the rain-fresh, Reece-free garden.

'Let's have that picnic tea we didn't get yesterday,' I tell Annie.

We rustle up dolly fairy cakes and teddy-sized chocolate chip cookies, cutting out the dough with the screwtop lid of a bottle to get them the right size for toy fingers.

'Smells like Mummy. I *love* Mummy. Where *is* Mummy?' Annie blurts, when the aroma of cookies baking starts to waft through the house.

I have to confess I know why this makes her feel sad. It's the smell of Mum being here, and, like Annie, I'm hungry to see her again. Luckily Annie's slightly more excited about seeing how her cakes'll turn out. So much so that she keeps trying to open the oven door before they're ready. I have to shoo her upstairs to dig out her toy teaset before I blow a gasket.

'Choose who's coming to our picnic. Make sure they're dressed in their best,' I tell her.

She's up in her room for ages, is Annie, although I'm too busy zipping about the place as if I'm on fast forward, getting things done before Annie undoes them, to notice at first. I've twenty daft things on the go at once: cutting up fruit for picnic punch, wiping up the carton of apple juice I spill all over the floor, searching our hut for a waterproof cloth to sit on in the garden, finding I have to scrape off mouldy traces of the last picnic we had on it a year ago, whipping my cakes out the oven just in time, daubing them with icing, Jelly Totting them. In the middle of everything I've to thole Dad on the phone, from Manchester by this time:

'Yes. Everything's hunky-dory.'

'Yes. I know, Gran must be out for the day. I've been trying her too.' Liar!

'Yes. We'll both be fine staying here on our own tonight, Dad.'

'Yes. I'll lock up.'

'No. Not a dicky bird from next door. I don't even think he's there.'

It's all a bit frantic, but don't get me wrong, I'm well happy. Off the hook this time tomorrow, I keep telling myself. No more Annie-minding. I'll be a man of means. Pay packet burning a hole in my jeans. Able to donner to HMV on my ownio and while away an afternoon flicking through CDs I can afford to buy for a change. No chance of Reece chumming along with me. Bliss. No wonder I don't grudge Annie a bit of a party.

And it's lovely outside, the garden misty magical

with the sun burning the rain off the grass so it steams like dry ice.

'What's keeping you, Annie?' I call upstairs. 'Everything's ready. Come on down! Picnic time.' I get our happy song blasting through the house: 'Good Day Sunshine' by the Beatles. Makes me think about Mum being home again. She says it's her favourite song because she loves the way we all end up singing along to it whenever it comes on. You can't help it, Mum says. Even Annie knows all the words. Belts out the chorus louder than anyone, so we all crack up and let her sing solo.

So the silence from her room? That's weird.

'Annie?'

I'm on the stairs, tripping over myself to get there fast, and I *know*, I *know* before I reach her door –

He's with her.

He's slipped in.

Somehow.

Reece.

Disturbed Reece.

The Firestarter.

I freeze. They've both got their backs to me. Annie. Reece. Cross-legged on the floor. Next to each other, but not touching. Reece is slumped over himself, blue dread snakes sitting on his shoulders, their red tips like eyes, guarding him from behind. Glaring me to a halt. I don't know what to do.

Should I burst in? Snatch Annie. Run.

Should I dive in? Wrestle Reece to the floor. Pin him down somehow. Then run.

Or should I tiptoe into Mum and Dad's room? Captain Keith Sensible. Dial 999. Wait.

I end up doing none of these things. Just stand there: Inaction Man. The thing is, Reece and Annie aren't doing anything untoward. They're just chilling. Having their own picnic, as a matter of fact. All the dolls and teddies that I was waiting for Annie to bring into the garden are propped in a circle around Reece and Annie, her duvet spread out in the middle of them, set with plastic cups and saucers and plates.

'Cheers, m'dears,' Reece is saying, tapping his cup

around every guest in the toy circle until he reaches Annie's. He clacks his cup against hers so hard that if there had been liquid in it, it would have sloshed everywhere. That's about as dangerous as he gets.

'You make a lovely cup of tea, Annie,' Reece says, sipping air, then smacking his lips, his tone exactly the same as Stevie's when he speaks to my sister. Genuine. Kind.

Reece sighs deeply. 'I'm gonna remember this tea party when I go away.'

Annie rocks from side to side on her bottom before she replies, half-turned, listening to the music from downstairs. 'Ooood day sunshine,' she sings completely out of tune. 'Why you go away?' she interrupts herself to ask, throwing in with a careless shrug, 'Stay here. Me dove you.'

Hello! How long have you known this guy, Annie? I'm thinking. Isn't that just girls all over? Always ready to chuck their hearts at the bad guy. Story of my life.

Not that there's anything bad, anything remotely bad, in what Reece is doing at this moment. OK, so he's escaped from Mrs Duff's again, and broken into my sister's room, but I could hardly describe going round a toy tea party with an empty pot filling plastic cups with imaginary tea as criminal: 'A drop more for you, Mr Ted. What about you, Miss Spears? What's that? Oh, I know you don't take sugar. Bad for your spots.'

That's why I let Reece be. He's harmless like this and, anyway, I'm here, the spy in the doorway in case anything goes wrong. All I have to do, when I want Reece to go, is burst into the room, kidding on I've just discovered him. 'Why didn't you tell me Funny Boy was here?' I can scold Annie. 'Daddy's going to be *very* cross with you. You'd better not say you were playing with him. We'll all get into trouble now, especially Funny Boy. And you wouldn't want that. Because you dove him!'

And Reece'll be gone tomorrow. I'll never see him again, I'm thinking, smug, as the music stops.

'Ooood day, sunshine,' Annie whisper-sings a couple of times. Then suddenly she catches her breath, and silence clangs through the house like an alarm shrilling. Quick, nervous, Annie tugs the sleeve of Reece's T-shirt.

'All quiet,' she says, expecting Reece to turn and speak to her. Like I would. Or Stevie, or Stewball: *It's OK, Annie.*

When Reece ignores her, Annie looks over one shoulder, then the other. Scrambles to her feet, backing away from Reece as if she's sussed that the change of atmosphere in the house is his fault. She doesn't see me. Well, she wouldn't, would she? I've shrunk into the darkness of our landing, hiding. Useless lump of yellow cowardy custard that I am.

'Teef?'

Annie clatters downstairs calling my name. She goes into the kitchen. The sitting room. Bangs on the downstairs loo. Hollers in the garden, her shrillness swooping back up to me from outside.

'Teef!'

I don't respond. I don't know why. Even when Annie stops calling out for me; gives it *Mummmeeee* instead.

See, I'm watching Reece. Can't take my eyes off him.

He's still sitting on the floor, crouched over himself like all his bones have melted. He's hugging his arms to his shoulders. His head's slightly cocked. 'Shhhhh. It's OK, Annie,' his voice soothes, 'don't cry.' He starts to rock backwards and forwards as he speaks, rocking harder and harder the louder and louder Annie wails.

'Mummeeeeee!'

'Don't cry. Don't cry. I know. I know,' he chants. Rocking. Rocking. Then suddenly he leaps to his feet, clamping his hands to his ears.

'Is that weed not gonna help her?' he hisses, and before I realise he means me, Reece is tearing past me, into my room, where I hear him banging my wardrobe doors open. Then he's running downstairs. Outside.

'It's OK, Annie, I know your mummy's not coming home, but I'm here now. And, look, Raggy's back.'

* * *

They're sitting on the garden steps, heads close, giving poor butchered Raggy the once-over when I put in an appearance. Before I joined them I'd picked up the phone in the hall, punching the number Dad had left for Mrs Duff. No one answered, and while I let the phone ring and ring, I debated whether or not to stuff Reece bigstyle by calling the cops. Have him arrested. I do nothing, of course. Dialling 999 seems totally OTT. After all Reece is only trying to feed poor Raggy one of my Jelly Tot cakes.

'I don't think her appetite's back yet –' he's telling Annie, in his sing-song voice. She's stopped crying. In fact, she starts laughing her head off when Reece shoves three cakes into his own mouth at once, then tries to speak.

'– cos these are magic, Annie. Did you really make them yourself?'

'Me help Teef –' Annie starts to say, chuffed to bits with Reece's compliment, but Reece cuts her off by putting the flat of his hand up to her face. He stands up, eyes narrow. He's clocked me coming outside.

111

'Where you been, mate?' Reece sprays cake crumbs like bird-shot as he moves towards me.

I pray he doesn't hear the tremor in my voice when I ignore his question. Point to the fence.

'You need to leave. Right now,' I say, hoping I sound firmer to Reece than I sound to myself. Clearly I don't. Reece comes so close to me that I can count beads of eyeliner between his lashes that he hasn't cleaned off properly.

'Annie was crying for her mum again, mate. You just left her.' Reece shakes his head, slicing my cheeks with the tips of his dreads. The smell of his hair's in my nostrils. Dirty, oily, smoky. 'They used to leave me crying like that after *my* mum . . .'

Reece glances over his shoulder at Annie – she's busy force-feeding Raggy a chocolate cookie – like he doesn't want her to hear him. His voice has dropped, barely a whisper, yet he's still moving closer. His hand reaches out for my wrist. Grips. Squeezes so I can't move, and his face is so near I can smell my own home baking on his breath. He's going to kiss me or Glasgow kiss me. I gulp, bracing myself. But all Reece does is whisper in my ear.

'You shouldn't leave her to cry when she's sad like that, man. You end up doin' . . . doin' *things* you don't even know you're doin' to make people come. You don't want that –'

'Don't want what? Annie's not sad,' I say, and a puzzled look spreads over Reece's face. He's looking from me to Annie, his grip on my arm relaxing enough for me to snap free.

'I want you to go,' I say, reaching past him to grab Annie. 'We're going in now.'

'No!! Mummmeeeeee!' Annie shrieks in my ear, belting me about the face with Raggy. 'Me play with Funny Boy. Hate you, Teef. Mummm*eeeee*!' she screams, stretching her arms out for Reece as I bundle her towards the back door.

That's when I lose it completely.

'Shut up, Annie. You're a naughty girl,' I snap, knowing I'm squeezing Annie's legs tighter than I should be.

'Mummmm*eeeee*!' Annie bellows over my shoulder, straining to leap up and out of my arms. No chance, I'm thinking. Until I feel a tug. Reece is behind me, trying to pull Annie away.

'You're sick, man. She's hurtin'. You'll screw her up, man. Let me talk to her,' Reece shouts. His elbows are digging into the knobbly bones at the top of my shoulders, weakening my hold on Annie. I feel her slipping from my grip into Reece's open arms.

'Shhh, shhhh, Annie. I know you feel bad.' As if I don't exist, Reece carries Annie over to the picnic mat and sits down with her, cupping her in his lap. Gently he begins rocking her back and forwards. 'I'm gonna be here if you want me,' he lulls her in his sing-song voice. 'I'll run away from my new place and visit you, I promise. And when I'm sixteen, I'll find work round here and we can –'

'Annie, if you don't go inside now, I'm telling Mum how naughty you are,' I interrupt this rubbish I do *not* want to hear.

'Aw, now you're *totally* sick, man,' Reece moans.

He buries Annie's head in his stringy blue hair, covering her ear with his hand.

'Hate you, Teef,' Annie chips in without lifting her head. 'Me tell Mummy you a big fat *poo*.'

D'you know what it's like when wee kids get really mad and blurt out something completely ridiculous? It's hilarious. Well, *I* think it's hilarious. Maybe I *am* sick, just like Reece says, but I can't help it. Here's Annie, wrapped in the arms of a weirdo firestarter that I can't get rid of, and I'm laughing my head off.

'Big fat poo, am I, Annie? Wait till Mum hears that. In fact, I'm gonna phone her and tell her right now.'

'No. Teef!'

'I'm gonna phone her. No, even better, I'm going to paint all over your banner and hang it outside the house: "Welcome Home, Mum. Annie called me a poo."'

I should have done something daft like this in the first place to make Annie laugh. She'd have listened to me over Reece long before now if only I'd lightened up a bit. Now I just need to throw in a burst of my spongly running on the spot to give Annie the chance to overtake me and – BINGO! – she's safe in the house before Reece even susses she's not sitting on his knee any more.

When only the pair of us are left in the garden, Reece rises slowly to his feet. Finding a toehole in the fence to boost himself, he begins to climb back over on to Mrs Duff's side.

'Her mum's not dead. Your mum's not . . .?' he's saying, although he's not looking at me. He rubs his forehead as if it's hurting him, puzzlement in his voice. At the top of the fence he perches, calls down to me before I go inside. 'Man, I thought there was so much we . . . thought we were mates . . . thought I could stay here and everything would be . . .'

His voice fades out like a song ending and I see he's doing that flappy thing with his hand again, passing it back and forth between us same as he did the day he found out my name was Keith. The day he torched Mario's. When he thought we'd all sorts of stuff in common.

Aye, right, I answer Reece Anderson in my head, watching him disappear over the fence. I cheer inwardly when he's gone, trying to pretend that I didn't notice he'd taken Raggy over the wall with him again.

Saturday

I wake up coughing. It's pitch black. Totally pitch black. Can't even see shadows in front of me and I have to put my fingers to my eyes to check they really are open. I've gone blind, I'm thinking, groping to my feet, starting to panic. Then I realise that I've been coughing in my sleep for a reason and I wasn't just dreaming that I smell burning. In fact my lungs are sucking and sucking in the same foul air that has turned my room so dark, without my efforts catching one clean breath. I fumble in bare feet from wall to wardrobe, trying to figure which way I'm facing, trying to find the door. 'I have to get out,' I hear myself wheeze. 'Have to get out.'

That's all I know for certain.

Because Annie isn't crying.

I'll come clean. I nearly shut myself back into my room when I open my door and step onto the landing, because I smack against this thick black wall of smoke which sears my mouth and nostrils when I breathe in. 'Annie,' I try to call, but my throat feels closed and only a rasp escapes. It's even darker on the landing than it was in my room and I have to grope along a wall to reach Annie's bedroom. By now my head is spinning, ready to explode from lack of oxgyen.

I stumble into Annie's room, arms stretched in front of me like a zombie, and immediately I fall hard on something large and stiff, all arms and legs and pointy boobs. Britney, sprawling where I dumped her when I cleared away Annie's tea party. Scrambling to my feet, my hands lean on Annie's window ledge and before I've even thought about it, I'm using Britney's head as a battering ram to smash the glass.

Fresh air. Fresh. Air. Just enough wafts through Annie's window to revive me a little, although there's smoke everywhere. Flames too, licking the sky ahead through a sooty black filter. 'Annie,' I croak, sticking my head outside for a gulp of oxygen before I dive back through the choking smoke for my sister.

Annie.

She's on the bed. Face down. Raggy limp. Not a squeak when I scoop her up, shake her and dangle both our heads outside the window. 'Annie, wake up,' I splutter, as smoke swirls in and out her broken window. It cloaks all traces of faint dawn light beyond, leaving me gasping to breathe again, leaving me wondering how the heck we're going to get out of here alive.

I can't go through the house. Can't risk groping through those fumes – flames too, probably – with Annie already unconscious, fumbling at doors I locked and double-locked when I went to bed, rummaging for keys I hid in drawers. We'd never make it. The only way out is the way Reece must have come in yesterday. Through Annie's window. One floor up.

* * *

You hear about people jumping out of burning buildings, leaping for their lives, falling to their deaths. What must be going through folk's minds before they jump, I've wondered. Well, let me tell you, that moment before you leap – it's incredible how many thoughts can cram your head. Well, mine anyway. I'm crawling out over broken glass on to Annie's window ledge and my head is buzzing:

What if I drop Annie and she smashes on the ground below?

It's concrete down there.

Maybe we could wait a minute or two, out on the window ledge.

I'm shouting HELP, after all.

Mrs Duff, the other neighbours, they'll hear.

Surely.

They'll drag out mattresses.

Guide my jump: *Left a bit. Right a bit. You're doing fine, son.*

If I just leap into the dark with Annie, we'll both

lie down there bleeding.

Paralysed.

Who knows for how long?

Worse, I might land on Annie.

She might break my fall.

I'd crush her and survive.

Couldn't handle that.

Maybe I should wait just a few more seconds on this window ledge.

Somebody's bound to smell smoke and call the Fire Brigade.

Because I can't jump.

It's too scary.

But I don't want to burn alive.

I'm thinking all this stuff, seeing Mum and Dad and Gran in my mind's eye, their faces being told their kids are dead in a fire, and I know – for Annie's sake more than my own – that I have to jump. But I can't. I shrink, I whimper, coughing, 'Help,' eyes streaming with smoky tears.

Then I hear a voice I know.

Sing-song.

Calm.

Close.

Very close.

'It's not that far to the ground,' says the voice. 'I'm up the drainpipe to your left. It'll take your weight easy. Come *on*.'

A hand grips my arm. Yanks me sideways from the window ledge so I lurch – off balance – into space. I tell you: the expression people use, about your heart being in your mouth? I know *exactly* what it's about. That moment of free-fall between ledge and drainpipe is the most terrifying of my life and it's all I can do to keep Annie gripped in one arm as I tip sideways, guided through the smoke by the sing-song voice.

'There. Don't say I'm not good to you, Teef,' says the voice when my arm is firmly hooked round the drainpipe. 'Plenty of footholds, though it's more of a blast to slide all the way. Pretend you're on a fireman's pole. Wheeeeeee . . .'

The voice is no longer close. Underneath me, I think, although, like a caterpillar with vertigo, I'm too busy edging my way downwards, Annie cradled over one shoulder, to pay much attention. A few feet into my descent Annie stirs in my arm and gives a tiny cough. When I hear that I don't need anyone's help to make the final journey to the ground.

Broken glass from Annie's window cuts into my bare feet as I land but I feel no pain. Knowing the gate to the street is double-bolted (on Dad's instructions), I run up the side of our house into the back garden. At Dad's hut I turn on the outside tap full blast and hold Annie lengthways underneath the water until she's gasping and wriggling to escape the cold stream. Whether or not that's the right thing to do, I don't know. And I don't care. All that matters is that Annie's alive; coughing, retching, crying when I put her in the recovery position and cover her with an old sack from the hut. All those people yelling and trying to kick the side gate open can take over now.

I crawl under the garden tap myself and dunk my

head. I'm dizzy, breathless, gagging. Bitter smoke fills my mouth, and stings my eyes. Spitting black phlegm, trailing snot, I turn to face my burning house.

Except it isn't burning.

Isn't on fire at all, as far as I can see. No flames engulf it, only smoke, belching round Annie's window.

The fire's next door, at Mrs Duff's, where orange flames are shooting from the roof. Licking the daylight sky.

'Score,' chimes a voice above me. Reece. He's perched at the end of our fence, almost hidden by the overhanging fruit trees at the bottom of Mrs Duff's garden. Both arms raised high in the air, he bends his elbows and punches upwards, as if he's holding an imaginary scarf . A gesture of . . . well, I have to say he seems to be having a ball to himself, rocking the fence from side to side and whooping, the way you would do at a concert, or a brilliant football match. When one great flame crackles along the wooden facing of Mrs Duff's roof and brings it crashing down on to the far end of our fence, he cheers.

Even though the fence is alight now.

'Ya beauty,' sings Reece, immediately groaning as three jets of water criss-cross and attack Mrs Duff's roof. 'Boo, let it burn,' he moans. 'It's magic. See how different everything is now, Teef?'

It takes a split second to click that Reece is speaking to me. I've my eyes fixed on our fence which is burning faster than a cartoon rope with dynamite on the end, flames gobbling the wooden struts one by one so the fence collapses against itself like a glowing deck of stacked, evaporating cards.

'You need to get down from there before you burn,' is the last thing I remember saying to Reece Anderson, way too distracted by everything else going on at that particular moment to know or care if he takes my advice. With the fence in cinders, I've an unbroken view of Mrs Duff, wrapped in a silver blanket, oxygen mask over her face. What the hell's happened to her? Where's her hair gone? What's wrong with her forehead? She's being stretchered from the shell of her house. She's wired to drips, swarmed by paramedics. Same as Annie, who's prised from my arms and rushed to hospital as a siren job. There's an ambulance team working on me, too. Checking my feet, my pulse, my airways. Telling me not to worry, lie still now. The paramedics think I'm thrashing about on my stretcher worried for Annie. Not trying to see what Reece is up to now that I've seen the state of Mrs Duff.

He doesn't hang around for long, swinging high into the branches of Mrs Duff's trees when the fire reaches the final struts of our fence. Would disappear easy along our back lane. But not before he waits for the head of the rag doll he's holding in one raised fist to catch fire.

Then he flings it at my feet.

Sunday

Mum's still freaked out. There was no one she recognised waiting to meet her when she skipped from the Leeds train yesterday morning happier than Julie Andrews returning to her long-lost children in the *Sound of Music*. Since Dad wasn't leaving Annie's side, the police collected Mum from the station. Broke the news that there'd been a bit of trouble. Whisked her off to the hospital.

No wonder she won't stop shaking when she comes in to collect me and hugs me so hard I think I'll crack. She says she should never have gone away and left us. She'll never do it again.

'I'm all right,' I keep telling Mum. And anyone else who'll listen. All that's wrong with me is a raging sore throat, a smoker's cough, cuts to my feet and snot the colour of which I will not describe. Even when they brought me in last night, I kept telling the doctors and nurses I was fine and I'd be even finer if they'd let me see Annie, but no one paid any attention to me. Insisted I spent a night under observation.

As soon as I'm discharged today, Mum and I bomb to the children's Intensive Care. *Your sister's very poorly from the smoke she breathed in* was all anyone would tell me. This morning she's still sedated; 'stable', a mini version of the oxygen mask Mrs Duff wore last night drowning her face. Tiny, she looks, her hand like a baby starfish curled up in my dad's palm. He won't let her go, even when he's holding Mum's hand as well, telling her over and over he should never have flown to Manchester. He'll never leave us again. Seems to mean what he says because he won't even leave the hospital to take me to the police station to make a statement.

'They've got their nutter in custody,' he says. 'Let

them come here and see what he's done so they make sure they throw away the key when they prosecute him.'

Eventually the police send over one of the officers stationed round the clock at adult ICU waiting to speak to Mrs Duff when she recovers consciousness.

The lady's in a very bad way, Sergeant Nora, the officer, tells us, trapped for hours before the fire crews reached her. She'd been locked in a bedroom. Tied up. Gagged.

While Reece Anderson was next door playing with my sister as if everything was hunky-dory. I only just hit the paper spew hat in time; panic literally surging up my throat. *I could have stopped this but I kept giving Reece another chance.*

'I tried to phone Mrs Duff to say Reece was in our garden,' I tell Sergeant Nora between retches. 'She'd have heard it ringing, not able to answer.'

'It was touch and go if she'd make it last night.' The sergeant shakes her head. She wants me to remember the exact time I phoned Mrs Duff. Jogs my memory by telling me she's suffered twenty per cent burns. 'Legs, mainly. She'll need skin grafts. *If* she wakes up. We could be looking at an attempted murder here, Keith. That's why we need as much information as we can get about Reece Anderson. He can't be doing anything like this again.'

I'll admit I'm pretty upset reliving what's been going down. Can't look Mum in the eye.

'I *knew* there was something wrong with you whenever I phoned,' Mum finally erupts when I'm done with my statement. She's on her feet, fit to be tied, keeping hold of one of Annie's hands, gesturing wildly between me and Dad with the other: *How could either of you let this happen?*

How *could* I let this happen? Why didn't I knock it on the head? I can't even explain it to myself. Is it really any excuse to say that most of the time Reece didn't seem *bad* in any way. Just off the wall . . . Different. And he was so decent with Annie. And she seemed to trust him. From the way he treated her I couldn't believe he was capable of what he hinted at, even if I did suspect he was dangerous . . . or sick.

'He even turned up when I really needed help. Led me and Annie to safety,' I find myself saying aloud, adding quickly before Mum starts up again: 'But I don't care. I don't ever want to see him again.' I'd better admit I'm in tears by now. 'I'm sorry, I'm sorry, I'm sorry.' Crying to Mum, Dad, Annie – especially Annie. 'I couldn't keep Reece away. I tried. Kept telling him to leave us, but he wouldn't go. This is all my fault.'

Since neither Mum nor Dad jump in to contradict me, Sergeant Nora hunkers down. When she tells me to listen good and pats my hand, she makes me cry even harder. No one's cross with me, she says, frowning at Mum and Dad like she's warning them off giving me a rollicking. It's Reece Anderson they're interested in, she says, and for what it's worth, his involvement with me has given the criminal justice system the breakthrough they need.

'We've pinned him down at last,' Sergeant Nora tells Mum and Dad.

Apparently when Reece heard how badly Annie was affected by smoke inhalation he owned up to starting last night's fire. Because his actions were so serious the cops charged him with wilful fire-raising for starters. He'll be held in some secure unit until he's tried through the adult courts.

'Reece has been a slippery fella to deal with. Out of the loop. Turns out there's a pattern of fires involving people he gets to know. Though nothing proven.' Sergeant Nora shrugs. Then with some pride she straightens her uniform jacket. 'But we've nailed him now.' She grins, until Mum bursts her bubble.

'Am I hearing you right? That boy has done *this* kind of thing before?' Mum's sweeping her hand around the room. Taking in Annie, still as marble beneath her mask on the bed. Dad, face slumped in his hands. Me, tear-streaked, juddering. I'm as surprised as the sergeant when Mum pipes up. Thought she'd stopped listening, unmoved by my tears, too busy trying to whisper Annie awake, stroking her forehead. Now I don't think I've ever seen my mum look so mad. She's crying too, her hand shaking as she smoothes Annie's curls away from her face. 'Why wasn't a boy like that being supervised properly?' Mum asks.

'It's complicated –' begins Sergeant Nora.

'Complicated? Paa!' Now it's Dad's turn to chip in. 'What's complicated about keeping tabs on a lad that's been starting fires since he was six?'

'Six?' Mum's voice is shrill enough to make Annie twitch within her deep sleep. Dad watches her, voice low.

'So I've been told now. The law knew all about this Anderson boy. Mother died when he was four. Left him and a sister. No dad. Some aunt took the sister, but Anderson went into a home. Then the aunt's place burnt down. Sister died from the smoke –'

'Like Keith and Annie could have done.' Mum's eyes are wide.

'Whatever you've heard off the record, can I just

say the police down south never proved anything, sir,' the sergeant interrupts. 'I mean: six years old? Committing a crime like that? I doubt it.' She shakes her head, gives another of her shrugs, hint of sympathy creeping in when she adds, 'Some roll of the dice Reece Anderson's had, eh? Never met the lad myself but apparently when you speak to him, he just doesn't seem capable . . .'

'Enough,' says Mum, holding up her hand like a traffic policeman. 'I don't want excuses. We can all make choices about how we behave unless we're sick in the head, and if this boy is sick, then someone who isn't should be looking after him so he can't harm other people. Look what he's done to my daughter, and my son,' she goes on, cranking up the volume in the little room we're crowded into so loud that Annie opens her eyes.

Life after Reece

By the time Annie's allowed to leave the Sick Kids'
hospital, days after the fire, her side room is fluffier
than Girlie Heaven. How anyone can nurse her!
There isn't a surface that doesn't scream pink, with
frothy, glittery, feathery, over-the-top kitschy gifts
and cards being delivered round the clock by all my
soppy schoolmates. They're desperate to outdo each
other and be the first person to make Annie pick up.

Then there are the flowers. Mum and Dad's
friends keep sending them. The goodwish messages
that arrive with the bouquets make Mum bubble
nearly as much as when she listens to me reading out
all the crummy jokes Stevie and Stewball keep
posting in to try and make Annie laugh. Unfor-

tunately, the flowers irritate Annie's breathing. Fortunately, Mrs Duff says they cheer her up no end, the scented ones reminding her of the garden when Mr Duff was alive. I take over a new bunch nearly every day to the main hospital. She doesn't have other visitors.

'Poor soul,' Mum always says when I mention Mrs Duff's name. She says it again today when I nip over to the Burns Unit before we leave the hospital with Annie. Since Mum's busy de-fairying Annie's room for the next sick child, Dad struggling to get Annie buttoned into a dress she says is pooey, I don't bother explaining, not for the first time, that Mrs Duff, despite the damage to her lungs and the burns to her legs, and the scarring on her forehead, isn't a poor soul at all when you get to know her. Mum and Dad wouldn't want to hear. To them, she's part of all the . . . well . . . what's happened.

Me? I actually look forward to going to visit Mrs Duff because she's a laugh, and I reckon, if things were different, she and Mum would really hit it off.

The two of them have the same sarky sense of humour, both sharp as tacks when they slag off the daft things that go on in the hospital. Like, as Mum says, the way the cleaners wake you up at the crack of dawn when you've spent half the night trying to get to sleep on your camp bed on the floor, and you've just dropped off.

'Or,' as Mrs Duff tells me the same day, 'the nurses turn the striplights on in my face and say, "Wakey, wakey, Sleeping Beauty." And me with all my hair gone and my eyebrows singed.'

See, she's decent, is Mrs Duff, not one bit miserable or sorry for herself. I mean, if I was her, I'd be whingeing off to everyone because I couldn't get on my feet. And I'd be totally cracking up to learn that while I'm stuck in hospital having all these lousy skin-graft operations, the bulldozers are in demolishing my house!

But Mrs Duff, she takes it all in her stride.

'You've lost everything,' I say.

'I'm still here though, amn't I?' she replies. Then

she smiles. 'And I'm well insured. Bill sorted that.'

'But where'll you live?'

'Moving up north when these skin grafts take, away from my noisy neighbours. Inverness. Sister lives there. She's younger than I am. Used to push her around. Now she can do it to me.'

Mrs Duff tries to chortle at her own joke, but ends up wheezing like a geezer with a sixty-a-day habit. While I wait for her to get her breath back, I remember something: Inverness. *He* lived there, didn't he?

'Your sister's Reece's gran?' I say, before I can stop myself.

Mrs Duff hesitates; nods, then shakes her head. She sighs and I wish I hadn't asked the question. I don't know what made me. It's the first time either of us have mentioned Reece's name since I first started visiting Mrs Duff. I know that must seem bizarre, given he's the only reason we're sitting together now in the hospital grounds: me, parked on a 'No Parking' bollard waiting for Annie and Mum to dish out

chocolates and kisses to all the nurses in Sick Kids;
Mrs Duff in her wheelchair. She wears one of those
grim-looking tartan blankets over her shoulders, and
her burnt legs stick out in front of her on a special
padded platform. Her raw scalp's as bald as a new-
born chick apart from a few bristly tufts of hair that
look as if they've been glued on her head for a joke.
Yeah, Reece is the only reason either of us is here,
but to be honest, he's never cropped up in our
conversations. There've been too many other things
to talk about: like Annie. Mrs Duff knows all about
her. 'Loved to listen to her chat through that big
fence your dad put up. I remember the day your
mum brought her home when she was born. Can still
see the look on your face. Over the moon.'

Mrs Duff seems to know plenty about me too.
'Bill and I used to hear you in the garden with your
friends. "Good lads," he'd say.'

Mrs Duff talks a lot about Bill. Not in a gloomy
way, though. He'd been a bit of a character, teaching
his foster boys to wrestle, to cook, taking every one

of them camping, even if they were only with the Duffs for a few days.

'Wonder how Bill would have managed Reece,' Mrs Duff says, now that I've brought up the subject. I'm wheeling her back to the ward because she says she's feeling the cold, pulling her tartan blanket tighter round her shoulders. Before I leave I have to tell her I don't know when I'll get in to see her again now that Annie's getting out.

'I'll try, but school goes back next week.'

'Don't you worry. You're a good lad.' Mrs Duff holds out her arm. When I give her my hand, she clasps it in both her own. 'And don't you go feeling guilty about anything, either,' she says. 'What's done is done. Put it behind you.'

Mrs Duff's advice is easier said than done! 'All this carry on' as Dad would say, means that the least of my problems involves bunking up with Stinky Sandy while our house is fumigated and we're all staying with Gran.

To be fair, I could have had it easy on that front, Stevie twisting my arm to stay with him. But I need to be wherever Annie is, part of the watch we're *literally* keeping night and day on her. She won't be brand new for a while yet. Listless. Too quiet. When she tries to speak her voice is hoarser than an Olympic shot-putter on testosterone; funny, then not funny when you know how bad she hurts. When you see how hard it is for her to breathe. When you think about how she nearly wasn't here . . .

Stevie can't get his head round that one. 'Keith, imagine if she'd died in that fire. Or been burnt, having to spend weeks in hospital like your Mrs Duff. Skin grafts, scars. I mean, wee Annie –'

'Quit,' I tell Stevie whenever he goes on like that. Like I need anyone to remind me exactly *how* badly injured Annie could have been! If I'm not actually thinking about it, it's because I've just forced myself to stop thinking about it, before I start thinking about it all over again. And then there are my dreams. I haven't told Mum or Dad this yet – they've enough to worry them – but every night I'm reliving the fire. Not the way it happened, either. It's worse than that. In my dreams I feel like I'm in one of those plays where the ending changes with each performance and even the cast doesn't know what's going on.

Sometimes Annie and I fall out the window.

Sometimes I scream and scream and Mum and Dad are there to scoop me and Annie to safety.

Sometimes I can't find Annie in that smoky bedroom. I grope every millimetre, holding my breath till my head pounds and I wake in the panic of a cold sweat.

Other nights Annie's burnt, her skin like melted doll plastic, sticking to my fingers when I touch her.

And then there are the worst dreams of all. I'm kneeling over Annie in the garden, trying to revive her with the hose, with CPR, and she stays limp . . .

Not the most Good Day Sunshine times I've known but at least Annie's getting there. Really picking up in the last few days. Bossing me, Stevie and Stewball round like the fem-sprog we know and love. Not once – and I don't know whether Mum and Dad have had a word with her, or if it's just because Stevie and Stewball are making such a constant fuss of her – has she mentioned Funny Boy. Or Raggy, strangely enough. Sandy, who's taken a real shine to Annie since we moved in with Gran, is her latest obsession. She's convinced he can be broken like a horse, and has Stewball, Stevie and me footering around his rank nether regions fitting him for a saddle and reins.

It's Stevie, demented with eczema from too much up-close-and-personal business with Sandy, who cracks first. He suggests the three of us chip in and buy Annie this fluffy horse with detachable wheels he's seen on e-Bay. Why he's looking up kiddie toys in the first place is a mystery I haven't probed yet, but he's made a good call. The arrival of Clopper brings the first laugh Annie's managed since the fire, not to mention kisses all round.

I'd been planning on buying Annie a new toy myself. Britney, who did her bit in saving both of us from suffocating, is poking, legs akimbo, from the mega-skip in our back garden along with all our other smoke-damaged belongings. Her head's wedged between Annie's bed and my wardrobe. Somewhere in that wardrobe droops the replacement Raggy from the posh toyshop. I never got round to introducing Marianna to Annie. Doubt they'd have hit it off anyway.

As for poor Raggy . . . I hope Annie forgets all about her. We find the doll, me and Stewball, face down in a sooty puddle at the bottom of my garden. Lying where Reece flung her at me.

I nearly puke when I pick Raggy up by the head, feeling the burnt stuffing inside squelch. Wet slime between my fingers. What's left of her dangling body falls away with a heavy shloop at my feet.

'Is that gagging or what?' says Stewball, with a shudder. Then he asks, 'How could you ever talk to a guy who did what he did?'

'I dunno.' I shrug.

Dunno.

I'm looking at the blackened pile of rubble that used to be Mrs Duff's house. It's a gap-site now, yawning like an ugly smile. State of the place hasn't put the property developers off, though. Four new flats going up in spring. Mrs Duff must be well pleased with the deal, Dad reckons. Diggers'll be in next month to clear anything away that used to stand here. Dad wants to get a new fence up quickstyle. The old one? Well, its black remains cinder a boundary between my house and Mrs Duff's. Last time I saw that fence upright, you-know-who was perched on it.

Reece Anderson.

Maybe you thought I'd shoved him to the back of my mind like Annie seems to have done. Filed him in a box I never need to look in again marked *Experiences that Taught me a Lesson,* along with poking a screwdriver into a live socket, mixing your drinks at Hogmanay, mountain-biking without a helmet and playing with fire.

Maybe you thought I'd forgotten about Reece altogether. After all, life's returned to normal. School's back. It's my first big exam year. I don't have enough hours in the day to cover everything I *need* to do, let alone dwell on something that's 'over and done with' (as Mum and Dad keep saying). I'm busy, busy, busy. No time to look back . . .

But who am I kidding? How can I forget Reece Anderson? He's everywhere, skirling through my life like invisible smoke. Those dreams I told you about? I omitted to mention that Reece is in them too: all black gear and make-up and chains. Remember I said way back that clowns are freaky? That you don't want them in your house? Well, take it from me: you don't want them in your dreams either. No wonder I'm peely-wally, as Mum says. She's got this habit of pressing apple-cheek Annie's face to my own to show

me how washed out I look. D⌐ ⌐
touch of Annie's warm skin only ⌐
lying pale on the grass; unconsciou⌐
revive her while Reece enjoyed the s⌐
top of our fence. Before I know it my t⌐
travelling from there to the memory of ⌐nie in
hospital. I'm stroking her face through the bars of her
cot. *Wake up, Annie, Funny Boy's gone.*

So now you know. Now you can see, he isn't
gone. I'm always thinking about him. The Funny
Boy. Reece Anderson. Even though I know he's
locked up rehabilitating in his secure unit 'miles from
any of us', as Mrs Duff writes in her first postcard
from Inverness.

'Good riddance.'

That's Mum and Dad's final verdict. Mum even
makes a show of washing her hands when she hears.

'That's that.'

But I can't scrub Reece from my own headspace
so easily. And it's not just because of the nightmare
he visited on me.

...hing is – and I can't tell Mum and Dad this in case they detonate, and I know it sounds crazy – but I worry about Reece Anderson. Not about him coming back, but about what'll happen to him. I worry about how he'll end up. How he'll manage without a proper family looking out for him. Will the decent side of him, the part that won Annie's heart, ever have any chance to thrive in captivity?

I worry about that.

And there you have it. As far as I'm concerned Reece Anderson's presence is being cemented in with the new foundations of the flats next door. I only have to glance from my window at the fence Dad's building and he's backflipping into my thoughts again.

Dangerous. Disturbing. Impossible to forget.

Like the vibe of that song he loves.

About the twisted Firestarter . . .